# One

After some struggle, the front door unlocks with its signature click—a sound that reminds me to take a breath and brace myself for whatever I might find on the other side.

I open it and scan my surroundings, noting how quiet everything is.

Slipping off my Converse, I walk across the foyer to the table I bought at an antique shop about a month ago. Antiquing is one of the few things that brings me peace. Wandering through unfamiliar towns, hunting for shops filled with aged treasures—artifacts, trinkets, forgotten relics of the past. I'm endlessly fascinated by how each piece holds a story, quietly carrying the lives of the people it once belonged to.

I have a thing for figurines. A whole collection stands proudly on a shelf in the living room, and I know they'll gain more companions as time goes on.

"Babe?"

Sorry. *Our* living room.

My fiancé turns the corner, and somehow, I manage a smile. He kisses me, and I kiss him back—softly. When he turns away, the smile fades.

"Dinner's almost ready," he says.

He isn't drunk. One night sober: his personal record.

This might actually turn out to be a good evening—though I'm not holding my breath.

I place the keys to my old Toyota on that same antique table—my favorite find—and run my fingers along its smooth edges, shaped decades ago by some unknown craftsman. I can still picture the store clearly: the warm, worn energy of the place, the old woman's knowing smile, and how nearly everything inside seemed to be made of wood.

Maybe I'll go back and visit.

Greg's arms wrap around me from behind, pulling my hands away from the table. The calming pull of the antique disappears, replaced by a sharp twinge of dread.

"Instead of caressing the table, how about you caress me?" he whispers in my ear.

I laugh shakily. "Sorry, Greg. I just really like that table."

"So?" he breathes, taking my hands and turning me around to face him.

Greg is gorgeous. Honestly, I still don't know how—or why—I ended up with someone like him. But, in the words of my best friend Betty: *'You're a lucky bitch, so deal with it.'*

His hands slip under my shirt, cold fingers sliding against the fabric, brushing my bare stomach—until the smell of something burning saves me.

I pull back. "Uh, your dinner."

He jumps. "Shit."

By now, it's probably obvious I've got some… uneasiness when it comes to my fiancé. Why? Well, his constant drunken state is a good starting point. But it's more than that. Something deeper is making me second-guess everything.

Is this the person I want? The life I want?

"You coming to eat?" he calls.

I head into the kitchen, suddenly cold.

Greg is gorgeous. He takes care of me—when he's sober.

And how often is he sober?

Tonight.

He's always talking about giving up alcohol, except, of course, for "special occasions." Weddings. Funerals. Tuesdays, probably. I'm still waiting.

I don't want to marry a drunk.

So why did I say yes?

I settle into one of our worn-down chairs and take a few bites of the store-bought lasagna when my phone rings in my pocket. I answer with the classic, "Hello?"

"Hey, you. Guess what?" Betty's voice practically sparkles through the line.

"What?"

"Phil proposed!"

I choke on my lasagna. Greg looks up, eyebrows raised.

"Uh," I stammer, standing and stepping out of the kitchen. "Wow. Really? He finally manned up?"

"Yeah! I can't believe it. We can have a double wedding!" Betty squeals.

I've known her since high school, and I can say with absolute confidence: she's never really grown up.

"Sure, Betty. But hey—dinner's waiting. Congratulations to you both!"

"You okay?"

"Yep," I say, trying to convince myself more than her.

I hang up and walk back into the kitchen. A tightness wraps around my chest, slow and suffocating.

"Who was that, Fran?"

I cringe. Every time he calls me that.

"Betty. Phil proposed."

"Honest to God? Well, good for them. I still scored the most beautiful girl, though." He winks. "Now eat."

I ate. But the lasagna tasted like cardboard.

---

"Here's to the happy couple!" Greg shouts, raising his beer bottle. The others cheer and follow suit, drinks high and sloshing.

Betty giggles, cheeks pink, latching onto Phil with a grin stretched so wide I swear it might split her face in two.

I wish I could feel that kind of sickening happiness.

"When's the big day, Greg?" Phil asks.

"We're thinking of next spring," Greg says, mid-chug on beer number three.

*We were?*

"Little Frannie must be super excited, huh?" Phil nudges me with his elbow.

*Frannie.* I might puke.

"I super am," I mumble, forcing a weak pun. The men laugh anyway, and I groan. The last thing I need right now is a frat party flashback.

I make my escape to the bathroom and sink onto the toilet seat, head between my knees. The dizziness rushes in like it's been waiting its turn.

"Fran? You in there?"

I blink. "No."

"Yes you are, silly. Let me in."

I glance around Betty and Phil's bathroom. I can't take any more engagements, any more wedding talk. And don't even get me started on kids.

"Go away, Greg."

He gasps. "Fran, you okay? Open up!"

I push myself up from the toilet and swing the door open. "What?"

Greg pulls me into a hug, his concern loud and theatrical. "Oh my God—since when do you cry?"

*Cry?*

My hands move to my cheeks. Wet. Tears. Actual tears. What is happening to me?

I shove him away. "Greg... I—I'm sorry. I just need to be alone right now."

I rush down the stairs, his stupid nickname echoing behind me. *Fran. Fran. Frannie.*

I burst through the front door and scan the driveway, locating our car among the clutter of others. I get in, fumbling with the keys, my heart pounding.

Where am I going? No clue.

But the moment I reverse, hit 40 km/h, my hands seem to know. They grip the wheel with purpose, and I let them lead.

Out of town. East.

And then—there it is. The small, crooked sign: *Dudsville*.

Underneath it, in faded spray paint: *"True to its name!"*

*Hooligan,* I think. Then pause. *Wow. Am I really that old?*

I drive through the modest downtown—quaint little shops lining the street like something out of a postcard.

My hands steer right, sliding into a parallel spot with unexpected precision. I sit there a second, mildly impressed. I may never pull that off again.

I get out and wander up the sidewalk, people brushing past, lost in their own errands and lives.

Then I stop.

Look up.

The bold red door. The sign above it, painted to match: *Granny's Treasures*.

*The store.*

I came to the store.

But... why?

I step inside.

The moment I cross the threshold, the energy wraps around me like a familiar blanket. My body softens. My lungs remember how to work.

I was holding my breath.

The little bell above the door jingles gently.

It announces a customer.

It announces me.

Someone emerges from the back room of the store.

It's the same woman—the one who had such a strange air of mystery the first time I was here. She's muttering to herself, rubbing her hands together like she's trying to spark a fire between them.

She looks up and studies my hesitant face. "Yes?"

She doesn't recognize me.

I freeze, unsure what to say. It's hard to explain why you've walked into a place when you're not even sure what you're looking for.

My phone vibrates in my pocket. A new iPhone—Greg insisted they were "all the rage." I ignore it, confident it's him.

The woman smiles, almost cautiously. "Excuse me? Are you alright?"

I step forward, honesty tumbling out before I can stop it. "No. I'm not alright."

Her light gray eyebrows rise with interest. "Hey… I know you, don't I?" She closes her eyes, searching her mind. Then, she opens them wide. "Wait—the English Edwardian demi-lune table, right?"

I nod. Warmth spreads through me—partly from being remembered, partly from remembering that table.

"That's me."

"So what brings you back today? And I sincerely hope your troubles sort themselves out."

I glance around: the worn wood beneath my feet, the rickety fan creaking overhead, the shelves lined with history. My gaze lands on the figurine shelf.

There's a new piece there—right in front, slightly off-center. Something pulls me toward it.

A woman, carved in Teak wood, dark and rich like mahogany. Her arms curve upward, elbows locked together above her head. A robe drapes around her body, modest enough to be tasteful, suggestive enough to stir curiosity. One leg is exposed in a graceful, almost defiant way.

"This," I say, almost in a trance. "I came for this."

The woman tilts her head. "I just put that on display today; it's been in the back for a while now. How could you have known about it?"

I lift it gently from the shelf and face her. "I didn't. Something's just… drawing me to it."

She exhales like she's been waiting for this moment. "That's actually one of my favorite artifacts. She's called *The Woman of Sin.* Always been a bit of a mystery."

"Mystery?" I echo, already knowing I'm not leaving without her.

"No one knows why or how she came to be. No history, no origin. She just… showed up."

She pauses, eyes glittering with something between wisdom and mischief.

"But I think she's meant for you."

A beat. Then she offers her hand.

"I think we're on good enough terms to share names. I'm Samantha Hedgeway."

I take her hand. "Francine Goodwin."

She smiles, her wrinkled hands taking mine gently as she gives them a shake. "Glad to have met you, Francine."

The smile wavers as a strand of gray slips from her updo. The lines around her eyes tighten, sharpening like a lens refocusing.

"There's something different about you, Francine."

I meet her penetrating green gaze—ancient, alert.

"Pardon me?"

She tilts her head slightly. "Can't quite place it, dear. I worked as a psychic for a time, and... I'm getting strange vibes from you."

"Weird?" I murmur, pulling out my wallet as I spot the price tag. Right. Reality—this thing isn't free.

She nods slowly and takes my money with care.

"Weird in a good way or bad way?"

That smile returns, gentler now. "Can't quite place that either. Have a nice night."

---

"Francine!"

I jump—though I knew Greg would be waiting. I was almost counting on it.

He's standing to my right, arms crossed, eyes lit with that blend of worry and rage that's become too familiar.

I offer a weak smile. "Hey."

"Where the hell did you run off to—with our car—for hours?"

I slip off my shoes, muscles aching with the kind of exhaustion that doesn't come from the body, but from the soul. My bag is slung over one shoulder, the strange wooden figurine resting safely inside.

As I move past him, I reply quietly, "Just went for a drive."

I place the figurine in the center of my shelf. She fits perfectly—like she's always belonged.

Greg follows, watching. "Where did you get *that*?"

"The same place I got the English Edwardian demi-lune table," I say, sounding more confident than I feel. "I ended up there somehow. Don't ask why."

He grabs my elbows—too hard. His dirty nails dig into my skin.

A flicker of panic rises in my throat. How many drinks in is he? Hard to say. Maybe *one* is always too many for Greg.

My heart races as he spins me to face him. "Fran, you think I haven't noticed? The way you've been lately? What's going on with you? *Talk to me.*"

His breath hits my face—stale and soaked in beer. That alone shuts me down.

Who wants to open their soul to someone who smells like broken promises?

I look at him. And yes, I *do* love him… or maybe I did.

But suddenly, all of it—his touch, his smell, his presence—feels like sandpaper on my skin. What is *happening* to me?

What's making me want to leave this place, this life, this *man*?

How do you explain something's wrong when you don't even know what it is?

"Greg, I don't know."

"How can you not know, Fran?"

"For starters, don't call me that."

He raises an eyebrow. "So you've been moody for weeks over a nickname?"

I groan. "Men. You can *never* talk to them." I escape to the bathroom, slamming the door harder than I meant to.

"Francine," he sighs—finally using my full name, like it's a peace offering. Guess he *can* listen when he wants to.

"Talk to me! Is it about me? Why did you leave Betty's place in tears? *Please!*"

Desperate to be left alone, I call back, "I'm taking a bath. Give me some time, okay?"

His face—confused, pained, and frustratingly loving—lingers in my mind as I twist the lock.

I turn on the tap, holding my hand under the stream as it heats up to skin-melting perfection. Baths have always been my sanctuary. Baths and ice cream. I mean, really—look at me. Living the dream.

I pick a bath bomb from Betty—last year's birthday gift. It hits the water like it's been waiting for this moment, spinning itself to pieces in a frenzy of fizz and foam. The water turns a deep rose red, and the scent of flowers fills the room.

I slide in, sinking beneath the fiery surface. Eyes closed, limbs weightless. The heat is almost punishing.

Red water, scalding temperature... it's kind of like I'm bathing in hell. Fitting.

A knock snaps me back.

"What?" I call, far less angelic than the bath bomb scent would suggest.

"Francine, your mom is here."

Oh, *perfect*.

I sink lower, as if the bath might swallow me whole. She is the *last* thing I need right now.

With a sigh, I pull myself out, watching the red water swirl down the drain. One final gurgle and it's gone—like the bath never happened. Like *I* never happened.

I throw on comfy clothes and towel-dry my hair. No blow dryer today. I don't have the energy to fake polish.

I open the bathroom door and there she is. Anne Goodwin, in all her "aged-like-a-real-housewife" glory, sitting at the kitchen table—laughing with Greg. Of course.

My mother has adored Greg since the moment I introduced them. She said he'd "set me straight," "put me on the right path." In other words, he was the man-sized band-aid for all the ways I didn't measure up.

Greg glances at me from over Anne's shoulder. My mother turns, red-lipstick smile blazing like a warning light. "Hello, dearest. Come here and give me a hug."

I oblige. She pulls me in tight and plants a kiss on my cheek, leaving a bright smear of lipstick behind. Cool. Not exactly what you want right after a bath.

"Mother, what are you doing here?" I ask, grabbing a paper towel and scrubbing the stain off like it's a bad omen.

"Can't a mother visit her only daughter?"

I snort. "That's the thing. You *never* visit. You're too busy hopping from one marriage to the next!"

Both my mother and Greg stare at me, mouths hanging open like I just threw a grenade. It hits me — I *snapped*. And I mentioned something I've never dared say out loud until now.

"Francine," my mother gasps, "What has gotten into you?!"

I open my mouth to defend myself — who else will? — but Greg cuts in, voice low but sharp.

"I've been trying to figure that out myself, Anne. Something's up with her. She's all closed off."

"She tends to be like that. It's not healthy."

*Whose fault is that, Mother?*

"Not healthy for her *or* for us," Greg adds.

I stand there while they talk like I'm invisible. Sometimes I wish I actually was.

I clear my throat. "Excuse me? I'm dealing with something right now, and... I don't even know what it is. So, can you just settle down, please?"

My mother turns, that fake sweetness creeping in. "Franny-cake, please."

*Clearly, my name has the absolute worst nicknames.*

"Mom, don't call me that!"

I turn away, and Greg's hands—his unmistakable touch—wrap around my shoulders.

"Fran, you're scaring me. I love you."

I turn back, hugging him tightly, hoping to calm the storm inside.

"I'm scaring myself too."

Suddenly, my mother breaks in, lifting her left hand to flash a massive engagement ring that sparkles under the kitchen light.

I swear, this year is the year of engagements. This will be her *fifth* wedding.

"Wow, congratulations!" Greg says, forcing a smile I know he doesn't feel. We recently had a long talk about my mother and her revolving door of men—back when things were... normal. I remember the connection, the wine, the laughter. What happened?

She beams. "He's the one."

I hug her quickly. "I'm sorry. Good for you. I hope he is."

"Anyway," she says, voice light, "our wedding's next month. You two are invited."

"I should hope so," Greg winks, making Anne's cheeks flush all over again.

She says her farewells and disappears down the driveway, but the expensive floral perfume she wears lingers like a stubborn ghost, filling the room long after she's gone.

"Well, would you look at that? She does it again!" Greg grins, turning back to me.

I shake my head, biting back the bitterness.

"Greg, why does she keep doing this? She said the guy after Dad was *the one*. That was... what? Three 'the ones' ago?"

Greg just shrugs like it's no big deal. "Some people just like collecting weddings like trophies. As for us? We'll marry and *stay* married. Right?"

"Right," I say, forcing the word like it's a rubber band stretched too tight.

He leans in and kisses me, slow and steady, then leads me toward our king-sized bed. Piece by piece, he peels off my clothes, and somewhere in the back of my mind, a tiny voice whispers: *You really need to figure your shit out.*

# TWO

"You've done it again," my Uncle Henry says from the stage, wrapping up his speech for my mother. He finishes with the usual well-wishes and forced optimism. I'm next up, and my mouth feels as dry as the savannah. I really don't want to do this.

"Don't fret, you'll do fine," Greg whispers, massaging my shoulders. "And did I mention you look beautiful tonight?"

I nod. Many times, in fact.

It's not nerves, exactly. I've recited a speech at every one of my mother's weddings—this is number four. At this point, I should have it down to a science. But I can't shake the feeling that it's all… a bit phony. The words feel required, not real. I want her to be happy, I do—but there's nothing original left to say. Every speech turns into a mad lib of predictable lines: *"You make me believe in soulmates." "You two look perfect together."* It's performative. And I hate being fake.

"Now, may I present to you Anne's only daughter and my niece, Francine!"

Polite applause. I step onto the stage, focusing hard on not tripping in these heels. I scan the room. So many guests for a wedding that was supposed to be "intimate." Her definition of small keeps expanding with every walk down the aisle.

Greg smiles at me from his seat, looking like his perfectly put-together self. My mother and soon-to-be stepfather are beaming at me with expectation. I take a breath.

"You're right, Uncle Henry. She's done it again." A few chuckles. "Love, as we know, is never simple. It takes years—and sometimes a few partners—to finally find 'the one.'"

I raise my glass toward the couple.

"So, here's to the one... and to finding them—eventually. I love you both."

The room collectively downs champagne. I open my eyes as the bubbly liquid slides down my throat and glance at Greg, whose gaze is fixed solely on me. I know I'm *his* one—but is he mine?

My heart constricts again. I quietly step down from the stage and head to the bathroom. In the mirror, my reflection stares back with frustration bubbling beneath the surface. I still haven't figured it out—this invisible force pulling me away from Greg, from marriage, from the perfectly paved road everyone seems eager to follow. Why can't the answer just be there, plain as day, pointing me in the right direction?

*If you say so.*

"Oh, crap!"

I gasp, turning toward the voice—and find a man sheepishly holding the bathroom door open.

"I swear, I'm not a woman," he blurts.

I burst out laughing—really laughing—for the first time in what feels like forever. I walk toward him, still chuckling. "Didn't think you were. Men's room is next door."

I study him without meaning to. Steel-blue eyes. Hair just light enough to flirt with blonde. He's got that clean, well-aligned smile that screams *middle school braces*, and a bit of stubble for good measure. Everything about him is fair, warm, sunlit.

Greg, by contrast, is all shadows and sharp angles. Dark hair, dark eyes, heavy brows.

Why am I comparing them?

He laughs too, pulling me out of the spiral. "You okay?"

I feel fresh tears on my cheeks and swipe them away. "Yeah. It's just… emotional. My mom's getting married and all."

His expression says *nice try*. He's not buying it, but he's polite enough not to say so.

"Well, if you ever want to talk about what's *actually* wrong," he offers, "I've got great ears."

He slips out into the hallway, and I follow, briefly distracted by his ears. They are, weirdly, kind of cute.

He flashes a quick smile and disappears into the correct bathroom.

And then—something hits me. A memory. No, not a memory. A *presence*.

I glance into my purse on a whim. The figurine. I've been bringing it everywhere. It brings… something. A lift. A lightness. A strange sort of comfort.

But now?

It's glowing.

White pulses of light ripple outward from it, fading fast. With each wave, the little spark of joy I'd been carrying shrinks. Fades.

**You should use me more.**

The voice is in my head—but it isn't mine.

I gasp and drop the figurine in terror.

Greg's hand lands on my back at that exact moment. The light vanishes. That icy wave of dread returns.

"Fran, what are you doing?"

I bend down slowly, slipping the figurine back into my purse like it's nothing. "Oh, just… went to the bathroom."

Back at the table, I blame it all on the wine. Sure. Too much wine. That's a safe excuse.

Betty bounces over with Phil trailing behind her like a duckling on a leash.

"Frannie, isn't this just the *most* beautiful wedding?" she gushes. "I mean, I *hope* mine is even better—but hey! You guys almost ready?"

She just *doesn't* shut up.

I throw my hands over my mouth, shocked by my own thought.

"Almost," I manage to say, blinking in disbelief.

"What she said," Greg echoes.

Everyone laughs—far more than necessary. I force a tight smile. Was that really knee-slappingly funny? I'm clearly missing something.

Suddenly, I feel it again. That hum. That strange pulse inside me. My gaze shifts—like being tugged by an invisible thread—and lands on *him*. The man from the bathroom. Out of nearly 200 guests, I find *him* instantly.

A soft white glow pulses from my purse.

**Go,** the voice urges. **Go get his number.**

And like a puppet on invisible strings, I stand. I cross the room toward him, drawn by something both foreign and familiar. He's doubled over laughing with a group of people I don't recognize. As I approach, he straightens abruptly, adjusting his tie like he's been caught doing something naughty.

"Come to check on me?" he teases.

I smile. "No. I came to talk. You said you have great ears, remember?"

His group raises their brows at each other and disperses with dramatic bows and smirks. He sighs.

"Don't mind them. I'm Ryan, by the way. I'm your new stepdad's cousin's friend," he says, nodding toward a guy chugging beer like it's his job. "He didn't want to come alone."

I nod. "Francine. The bride's daughter—but you already knew that. Listen... would it be too much trouble if I got your number?"

Ryan arches an eyebrow. "Not to pry, but don't you already have a suitor tonight?" He gestures subtly in Greg's direction.

"Oh, him?" I say, the white light now practically buzzing with encouragement. "He's a friend. And who says I can't make more?"

Ryan laughs—and it sends a strange warmth through me. There's a charm in it, like sunshine breaking through clouds.

*It's easy to lust after this one, isn't it?* The voice whispers again.

What the hell, figurine.

"More the merrier," Ryan grins, and inputs his number into my phone.

I feel my cheeks flush as the reality of what I've just done sets in. I walked over to a *total stranger*, flirted, got his number—and all while Greg is *right there*. Watching? Maybe. Hopefully not.

*Abort. Abort mission.*

"Well, thanks! I'll text you," I say, backing away like I'm escaping a crime scene.

Behind me, Ryan's friends are already making exaggerated faces at him. Careful, boys. If karma's feeling spicy, they might get stuck that way.

"Who was that?" Greg asks, his tone light, but his eyes scanning me for something.

"Just... someone I thought I knew," I reply, wondering why I'm lying so easily, so smoothly. Like I've been doing it forever.

Just then, the old woman from the antique shop resurfaces in my mind, her gravelly voice echoing: "She's called *The Woman of Sin*, and has always been known for her mystery."

Yeah, mysterious is putting it mildly. What's her endgame? Why can I hear her voice? And seriously, *Sin*? That's what we're calling her? The figurine's naming committee must've been feeling *bold* that day.

But I don't get much time to dwell. Greg grabs my arm and gently tugs me back to our table, where cousins I haven't seen since puberty are either glued to their phones or too drunk to know what year it is. I'd prefer to join the latter group, honestly.

Spotting my empty wine glass, I lean into Greg, "I'm going to get a refill."

"You'll find me on the dance floor," he says, already half-way there, beer in hand, fists pumping to a beat that clearly only he can hear.

I grin and turn toward the bar—and *bam*, the heat in my purse pulses again. Yep. We all know who that is.

I let it guide me, pushing past clumps of relatives in taffeta and too-tight tuxes, finally reaching the overworked bartender who looks like he's halfway to a nervous breakdown.

I wave. "Hey there, just another glass of your finest red."

He nods, sweating profusely, and slams together a couple of drinks before handing me mine. With a polite thank you, I retreat to the edge of the dance floor, observing the chaos.

Kids spinning in circles, parents pretending they aren't too old for the Cupid Shuffle, and somewhere in the madness—Ryan. Of course. Mid-gesture, he's mimicking some obscene move at his buddy, laughing like he hasn't got a care in the world.

I giggle despite myself and stroll over. "Surprised that move hasn't gone viral yet. Maybe it's the next Harlem Shake?"

Ryan turns with raised eyebrows. "The Harlem Shake is *so* 2013. This?" He points at his hips, "This move is eternal. Generational. Museums will want me."

I laugh again—real laughter—and raise my glass in mock admiration. "Best thing I've seen on this dance floor all night."

"You a dancer?"

I shake my head. "Definitely not. I drink. I observe. I get drawn in by ancient figurines... you know, the usual."

I stop myself. *Too much?* But Ryan just smirks, eyes twinkling like he's up for a little mystery too.

"Well, no one else here seems to be... other than me, of course," Ryan says, giving his hips a cheeky shake.

I roll my eyes, grinning despite myself. "Let loose a bit," I say, sliding into that classic side-to-side shimmy that screams *I'm pretending I'm carefree.*

Ryan watches and shrugs. "Better than nothing."

"There you are!"

Greg's voice cuts through the music like a record scratch. I turn and see him marching over, eyes fixed on Ryan with a look that could shatter glass.

Ryan, ever the gentleman, stops mid-shimmy. "Well, you must be her fiancé. Nice to meet you!"

Greg sizes him up like he's appraising a threat. "Yeah, well, thanks for taking care of her for me."

I sigh and toss back the last of my wine. Yep—definitely too sober for this caveman posturing.

"Greg," I mutter, "I'm not five years old, you know?"

Greg chuckles, that familiar low rumble that used to make my heart flutter. Now it grates like a squeaky door that never gets oiled.

"Never said you were," he replies, too cool and too dismissive.

I brush the baby hairs off my sticky forehead—those two defiant curls that have been tagging along since birth, now frizzed with disapproval.

"Sure, sure," I mumble, offering Ryan an apologetic smile. He just raises an eyebrow, half amused, half *yikes*.

"I'll let you be on your way," Greg says pointedly to Ryan, nodding once in that *alpha male dismissal* move that makes me want to vaporize.

Ryan lifts his glass in awkward farewell and turns away, disappearing back into the crowd, no doubt in search of his more welcoming friend.

"Follow me," I say through gritted teeth, heading toward the ballroom exit and into the blissfully cool cocktail lounge. It's quiet, open, and best of all—not a single person is trying to bump elbows with me to *Despacito*.

Weddings are dumb.

(*Says the engaged woman.*)

"Fran?" Greg's voice is soft now, trying to read me.

I blink, snapping out of my thoughts. "Sorry. Look… what was that all about?"

He tilts his head like a confused Labrador. "What was what all about?"

"Your whole *grr, me protect woman, you step back* act in there," I say, pointing vaguely toward the ballroom, as if I could summon Ryan back like Beetlejuice.

Greg frowns. "That poor, helpless soul didn't look so helpless when he was standing *this close* to you, drooling. And you let him."

*Oh boy.*

I groan, my hand reflexively touching the weighty engagement ring on my finger. I remember the night he gave it to me—how I gasped at the size, the sparkle, the impossible romance of it all. In that moment, I had no doubts.

In that moment, Greg was all I wanted.

---

*It was a warm spring day—the kind that reassures you winter has officially packed its bags and left town. Life was blooming, unapologetic and unconcerned with frostbite. I remember the smell: cut grass, budding flowers, sun-warmed skin just starting to sweat.*

"Francine."

*I turned, my frilly blue dress fluttering around me as Greg waved me back to our little* setup. Picnics were our thing—an unofficial tradition. New views, new snacks, new wine pairings. A curated kind of love.

"I brought your favourite," Greg said, shaking a bottle of Kim Crawford like it was a winning lottery ticket.

I smiled, settling onto the red blanket. "It's like you know me or something."

We clinked glasses and I let the wine coat my throat like silk. Yep. Definitely a second glass kind of day.

"Franny... this past year's been more than I could've dreamed of," Greg started.

I nodded slowly. This was our anniversary weekend. We missed Thursday because of work, so we stole Sunday instead.

"It's been fun," I said truthfully.

"So much fun that I'd be okay continuing to have fun forever... with you."

He dug into the picnic basket and pulled out a small velvet box. Blue. Of course it was blue. I choked slightly on my wine, then downed the rest for courage.

"Francine, will you do me the honor of being my wife?"

The ring sparkled like it had a PR team. Big. Flashy. A whole personality.

Greg's face was lit with that open, boyish joy that once made me feel safe. He'd be a good husband. A good father.

But... with the drinking?

"Fran?"

"Uh... yes!" I blurted.

He squeaked something unintelligible, slid the ring on my finger like he couldn't get it there fast enough.

"Greg?" I asked cautiously, staring at the stone now shackled to my hand. "Can you at least promise you'll consider going to AA? I mean... now that it's, you know, serious?"

His eyes hardened for a flash, then softened. The mask. "Of course, sweet girl."

---

I snap back to the present.

Greg's staring at me, eyes blazing. "Where the hell were you?"

I smooth the creases in my dress—funny, they're gone now. "Just... thinking. About when you proposed."

His eyebrows shoot up. "Why? We're discussing you hitting on a random guy. Don't you think that's more important than reminiscing?"

"I wasn't—I mean, I... I didn't..." I trail off, disgusted by how easily the lie escapes. I *hate* lying. Always have.

But Greg lying about AA? That was the first domino.

A familiar warmth pulses from my purse. It's her. The figurine. Comforting, urging. And then I hear it again, the voice, feminine and soft like wind through trees:

**Take a break from him. It's what you need.**

"Take a break?" I murmur, almost involuntarily.

Greg stiffens. "A break? From *me*?" His voice cracks with disbelief. "But... we're supposed to be planning our wedding."

"Exactly," I say, barely above a whisper. "Which is why... we should think about this."

His face turns crimson, fists clenched so tight his knuckles go paper white. "What's to think about? I proposed. You said yes."

"Greg, it's not that simple. There's so much *more* to it than that."

"You want *more*?" he snaps. "Clearly. With Mr. Big Ears back there."

"It's not about him," I insist, voice rising with emotion. "It's… I just don't know if I'm ready for *this*." I gesture toward the extravagance surrounding us. The done-up venue. The people. The expectations. "For all of it. For… you."

Greg looks like I just kicked his puppy, his voice trembling. "*Me?*"

"You won't even give up drinking for me. You won't even *try* to go to an AA meeting. I… just need some time to think."

"But—"

"*Franny, dear!*"

My mother appears, swaying in her over-embellished wedding gown like a ship caught in a tipsy storm. Her voice is just shy of a slur, but the champagne in her hand is far from her first.

"Yes, Mother?" I force a smile.

"Are you having a good time? Getting any inspiration for your own wedding?"

I sigh, but Greg beats me to a response. His voice comes like a dart laced in venom.

"The only inspiration she's getting is what other men she might be into."

He stalks off, surely to dive headfirst into another drink. My face burns hot. How incredibly humiliating.

**Let him go**, that now-familiar serene voice coos from the purse. It's soothing. Reassuring. A little *too* calm, considering it's apparently advocating for ditching my fiancé in the middle of my mother's third wedding.

Why does it want this? Why *now*? What could possibly be gained from dropping Greg like a sad canapé and flirting with someone new?

I've never been a cheater. Never even *looked* elsewhere. This isn't me.

Or… was that just the version of me that stayed quiet to keep the peace?

"Dear, what did Greg mean by that?" My mother's voice cuts back in.

I blink, the heat flooding my skin despite the foyer's chilled air. "He's just drunk. I mean, what else is new?"

She grimaces like she just tasted something sour. "Well… do try to have fun, dear."

Sure, Mom. My idea of fun is you giving me half of your wedding budget so I can book a one-way ticket to literally anywhere with no open bar and zero expectations.

"I will," I say instead.

The rest of the night is a blur of sweaty dance moves and predictable playlists. I sit, picking at the hem of my dress, watching Greg cradle beer after beer like they hold the answers to all his problems. If he's trying to prove why we *shouldn't* get married, he's nailing it.

"Did I get you into trouble?"

I jolt, spilling what's left of my wine onto the tablecloth. Of course.

Ryan stands there, all awkward charm, hands tucked into the pockets of his slacks.

"Want some help cleaning that up?"

I shake my head, dabbing pointlessly at the stain. "No, no—it's doomed. They'll either toss it or bleach it within an inch of its life. And to answer your question… no. You didn't get me into trouble. Greg and I… have things to figure out."

His brow furrows. He doesn't believe me. Not really. But he nods anyway. Polite. Respectful.

"Well," he says, stepping back a little. "I'll be heading out. I do hope to hear from you… sometime."

I manage a smile. It's small but genuine. "Sometime."

# THREE

The next few weeks drag on laboriously. For one, work has become more demanding than ever. As a radio talk show host, I recently discovered I give decent advice. Barry and the crew at the local news station, which is teetering on the edge, even coined my new 5 pm slot "Franny's Corner." Lately, I've been feeling a bit hypocritical—I dish out love advice to women and men alike, yet I can't even figure out my own messy love life.

And then there's Greg and me. Since my mother's wedding, we haven't really come to terms with anything. The silence between us is deafening as we go day to day, uncertain about our future.

"Franny-fran! Come on over!" Barry calls.

I wince, lowering my coffee mug from my lips, losing that sweet escape of hot amber liquid. I walk over to him, silently resolving to change my name. "Yes, Barry-bar?"

Barry bursts out laughing as if I'm performing stand-up comedy and pats my shoulder.

"You're too funny! Maybe we should rename your show to 'Jokes'… anyway, we just got the ratings for this month. Girl, you are lit!"

I can't help but smile at Barry's endless need to sound hip with phrases even I don't fully get. He points to a dirt-speckled chart on his screen—seriously, dude, clean your monitor. "See? Last month you were at 80%. This month? 90%! Keep it up, love!"

I nod, bringing my mug back to my lips and disappearing into caffeinated bliss. Barry glances at his watch—who even wears watches anymore when everyone has phones?—and notes, "You're on in ten! Go get settled. Our special guest will be here soon."

I turn on my heels; my small boots clack against the hardwood floor. Since the renovations, the studio feels more like home—as if we're one big happy family. Before, it was just concrete floors and oddly painted drywall.

I settle into my large red plush office chair, finishing the last of my coffee. What alcohol is to Greg, coffee and chocolate are to me.

Barry points to me—time to go live. Even after over a year on the show, the countdown always makes my heartbeat quicken.

As the number one disappears and the red light flickers on, I take a deep breath and begin:

"Hello there, my beautiful listeners! You've tuned into 'Franny's Corner,' where we discuss all things love, relationships, and our favorite topic: sex! Before we dive into calls and welcome our special guest, here's some daily inspiration for you: Be who you are and say what you feel, because those who mind don't matter and those who matter don't mind.

This is crucial because you can't truly love someone else until you love yourself. You need to understand who you are and what makes you tick before you can be someone else's partner. Partners work together to bring out the best in each other—excelling in life. But remember, you don't *need* someone else to complete or define you. You are an extraordinary human being capable of bringing so much to this world. Let yourself find out what that is!

Anyway, enough rambling from me. Let's meet our first caller—hello?"

Static crackles before a female voice cuts in, "Can you hear me?"

"Yes, I think I hear you now!"

"Awesome. I was so worried that after finally making it on the air, with my luck it wouldn't work!"

We share a genuine laugh. I smile, "Yeah, that would've been pretty unfortunate. So, what's your name?"

"Sandra."

"Okay, Sandra. What's your question?"

She sighs deeply, the weight in her voice unmistakable. "I… I think I like someone who isn't my husband. What does that mean?"

My heartbeat quickens, sensing the same confusion stirring inside me. "It usually means something's missing. Can you try to tell me what that is?"

"I… we don't really have sex anymore. Maybe that's it."

I nod, mentally crossing that off my own list. Greg definitely wants sex too often sometimes. "Lack of intimacy in a committed relationship can definitely cause problems over time. Have you talked to your husband about it?"

"I tried, but… he thinks sex shouldn't be such a big deal in a marriage."

"Everyone has different needs in a relationship based on their past. But this is *your* need, Sandra. He should be willing to work with you to find a compromise so you can both have a happy, fulfilling marriage—without infidelity."

Sandra's voice trembles. "Okay, I'm going to say something I've never said out loud before. Fran... that person I like who isn't my husband... it's a *she*."

I nod slowly, the real issue coming into focus. "Ah. I think I understand now. You're scared to admit your feelings for a woman. With how unaccepting society can be, I get why that terrifies you. Plus, you're married to a man. That must be so confusing."

She laughs nervously. "That's an understatement."

"Listen, Sandra. Divorce is never what anyone dreams about on their wedding day. But what's more important than anything else is *you*. We only get one life here—well, as far as we know. It's not easy to chase what you really want, especially when other hearts are involved. But would you rather stay in this marriage unhappy, making your husband unhappy too, not feeling fulfilled sexually? Or would you rather face some pain and hardship now, so you can come out free and ready to explore what you truly want?"

There's silence. As always, I take a moment to remind myself that I need to take my own advice more often.

Finally, Sandra whispers, "Wow, Fran... you're right, obviously. I'm just so scared—how my husband will react and how the world will react to my redefined sexuality."

"Those are things that will either make the journey harder or easier, but listen... you're going to look back on today and think about how this was the best decision of your life—as you lay in bed with a beautiful babe."

Sandra laughs. "Okay, okay. I'll do it. I'll talk to him tonight."

"Awesome. I wish you all the best. And remember: love yourself."

"Thank you, Fran! I love you!"

*Click.*

Barry raises his thumb high, giving me the seal of approval. I lean back toward the mic, "Well, there you have it. I never enjoy suggesting divorce and firmly believe in working through your issues together... but sometimes, it's clear someone will live a happier life elsewhere. Now, I've just been informed our special guest has arrived. He's a well-known relationship expert, here to answer your questions—along with me."

Barry opens the door and guides a man in a sharp grey suit into the studio. My breath catches—Ryan. The same guy from my mother's wedding.

*Excuse me, can I just pause life for a second?*

**No time, hun.**

I jump, recognizing the soft, familiar voice—but wait, I left the figurine at home today after sleeping through my alarm. This is definitely some weird magical hoodoo stuff. The statue's voice seems to travel through walls and streets, right into my head like a cellular signal.

Ryan catches me staring and raises an eyebrow in confusion but quickly settles into the chair, leaning into the microphone.

"Ahem... Hello, listeners! Ryan Steel here, coming at you live from Franny's Corner! I'm thrilled to be here today to help guide you amazing people onto better paths. I'm known for my bestseller, *To Love or Not to Love*, and have helped shape thousands of lives at my seminars. So, let's get started. Fran... how are you doing?"

I gulp, willing my spit to cooperate, "I'm doing great, Ryan. We're so excited to have you here today to share your wisdom. Navigating life and love is no easy feat, so we welcome any advice you can give!"

"Of course. How about we answer the phones?"

I nod and press the chunky button, "Hello?"

"Oh my God, hello!"

"What's your name, love?" Ryan asks, smiling like the woman on the other end can see it.

"Maggie, it's Maggie. Can I just say, you two together are perfect?! Fran, I've listened to you forever—you're so inspirational! Ryan, I've loved every one of your podcasts and seminars!"

"We're happy to hear that, Maggie. Our goal is to connect with all of you out there and remind you—you are not alone. Humans are complicated creatures with emotions galore, and no two are the same. So, Maggie, lay it on us!"

"I'm currently getting over a breakup. I'm used to breakups, unfortunately… I don't know if it's just my luck, or if my type is a bunch of dicks. But this one's different—he broke up with me for… my best friend."

I grimace as Ryan shakes his head slowly, running a calloused hand over his face. "Wow, Maggie, that must be so hard to deal with. I bet you've been having a hard time trusting people since, right?"

A sigh comes through the line, heavy and raw. "Yes, Ryan. How can I, when the two people I trusted with my life stabbed me in the back?"

I jump in, my voice soft but steady, "Maggie, that happened to me too. It honestly felt like someone grabbed my heart and ran it over. Even though it was in high school—with my first love—it still hurt just as much. I'm going to be honest with you: trusting people won't come easy right now, or at least not for a while. You need to focus on yourself, love yourself. You're a badass woman, and you have to believe that. By the time you've grown, you might find trust again. Think you can do that for me?"

"Y-yes, Fran. It's refreshing to hear the truth—that I will need some time."

"You're only human, Maggie," Ryan cuts in gently. "You need to feel these emotions and make sure you don't bottle them up. I know all too well how that ends... not well. Talk to your close ones."

"I will... thank you both! You'd be such a power couple," Maggie says.

I blush, realizing she's forgotten I'm currently engaged. Ryan laughs, thankfully jumping in again. "That's sweet, but from what I hear, Fran's taken." He shoots me a look, and I give a weak smile. He wraps up, "Thanks for calling in, Maggie. All the best, okay?"

"Thank you! Bye!"

Ryan turns to me, the question I've been avoiding hanging in the air. "So... what are the chances of this?"

My cheeks flush scarlet. "Slim to none, but here we are. How have you been since the wedding?"

Barry is making his way over, Ryan replying, "Pretty good. How about lunch? We won't have time to catch up here."

Nervously, I play with the strings on my sweater. "Sure, sounds good."

Barry opens the door, smiling wide. "That was amazing, you two! Ryan, we may ask you back—the ratings are through the roof!"

Ryan grins at Barry while I study his big ears. "Of course I'll come back, Barry. Fran is great company!"

Barry winks at me, nods, and closes the door behind him, leaving Ryan and me alone in the suddenly much smaller studio.

We come back on air after commercials and answer a few more calls.

"Hi, this is Fran and Ryan from 'Franny's Corner.' Can I have your name?"

A gruff, deep voice replies, "Yeah, you can. The name's Steve."

"Steve! What can we do to help?" I ask, secretly excited about a man on the line. Females usually call in, so this should be a nice change in perspective.

Steve growls, "Yeah, you can help… by not butting into relationships without any consideration for the other partner!"

I gasp as Ryan raises an eyebrow. Clearing my throat, I say, "Sorry, Steve?"

"You heard me," Steve snaps. "I had the pleasure of going through a divorce because you told my now ex-wife to 'be true to herself.'"

Honestly, I always figured it was only a matter of time before something like this happened. A lot of relationships end after my advice—sometimes for the better—but someone was bound to push back.

"Listen, Steve… I get it. Finding out your wife left you because of some stranger's advice has to be infuriating. I offer guidance, never condone divorce. I believe in working through problems. But how about you help me out here? Why did she want to leave?"

A pause. Then, "Well… that's not important."

I press gently, "I think it is. I talk to a lot of people, and I want to make sure I didn't overstep."

Steve sighs. "I strayed a few times. I felt unfulfilled… different." His voice trails off.

"So you cheated on your wife?"

"Yes," he admits gruffly. "I was confused. I get where I went wrong, but to find out it wasn't even a decision we made together… it was some radio personality's push? I just felt like you interfered with a huge decision in our lives."

"Yes… I definitely influenced her decision," I admit. "But listen, I care about people's happiness and living their best lives. Now, you can explore that unfulfilled feeling and find fulfillment, and she can find someone who's fulfilled with her. Right?"

"Right. It's just… it's still fresh."

Ryan jumps in, giving me a break. "Steve, it's Ryan. We know our advice can help—and sometimes hurt. We take that responsibility seriously and we're truly sorry you, and anyone else, has been hurt by it. But look at it this way: it might sting now, but you'll both find a happiness you didn't have together. Things run their course, and maybe Fran pushed you to end it sooner than intended—but are you happier now?"

"Y-yes."

"That makes me really happy, Steve. Keep chasing that fulfillment, and don't hesitate to reach out if you ever want to talk."

"Thanks… you too."

Click.

I stare at Ryan. "Wow… did that just happen?"

Barry bursts through the office, papers flying off desks. "You guys handled that like pros! You okay?"

We both nod, and Ryan shrugs. "It's expected in this line of work."

Barry grins, "Go get lunch, you two."

Barry heads off toward his office, but not before stopping at the coffee station. I grab my sweater, feeling my pulse quicken in my wrists and chest. Ryan nods toward the door for me to follow, and I oblige. He holds the door open, and we stroll down the block to a quaint lunch spot, full of southern charm.

Ryan seems calm, cool, and collected as he takes a seat opposite me, flashing that wide smile.

I definitely do *not* feel calm, cool, or collected.

"So… fancy running into you so soon after the wedding," he begins, glancing at the waitress behind me as he gets ready to order.

"Yeah. If I didn't know better, I'd say you were following me," I say, trying to inject some humor. He smiles, clearly liking the jab.

"You caught me. You left quite the impression, Fran."

I fight back the blush slowly spreading across my cheeks and the bridge of my nose. He makes me feel like I did back in Grade 9 with my first crush, Oliver — hiding behind my locker or my friends every time he glanced my way, cheeks burning with that familiar heat.

"Yeah, I figured you'd be into a woman who fights with her fiancé *and* her mother at a wedding."

Ryan shrugs. "I don't have the best relationship with my mother either. No judgment here."

Before I can ask more, the waitress arrives.

"Sorry for the wait, lunch rush," she says. "What can I get you to drink?"

Her faded name tag reads *Penny*. Big, bouncy raven curls — the total opposite of my thin, lifeless red hair — and bright blue eyes that lock onto Ryan as he orders a simple black coffee. Why can't she remember *just* a black coffee?

Her gaze lingers on Ryan an extra moment before shifting to me. "And you, ma'am?"

*Ma'am?* Who still says that? Society clearly hasn't gotten the memo that word can be a minefield.

I feel a flicker of jealousy and annoyance creep up. "Coffee as well, but not black. Milk and sugar, please."

She nods, jotting down the easy order. "Awesome. Be right back."

How can I be jealous of a man who isn't even mine? How can I feel jealous when I'm engaged to someone else?

**Maybe you're with the wrong one.**

The voice — *that* weird inner voice of the figurine — whispers again. I swallow hard, heart pounding. Just as I start to chalk it up to exhaustion or a strange dream, it returns.

Ryan checks his phone as it lights up but doesn't answer. Instead, he looks back at me. "Sorry, what were we talking about before Penny came by?"

Greg would have answered immediately, making me wait.

"Just… that you don't have a great relationship with your mother either. I wanted to ask what happened but didn't want to pry. Also, the fact that Curly came."

"Curly?"

I blush. "The waitress. Did you see her hair?"

Ryan laughs. "Oh yeah. Not sure how she manages that mess."

*Mess?* So maybe he actually prefers thin, lifeless hair over big, healthy locks?

"Right?!" I agree way too enthusiastically.

Ryan clears his throat. "Anyway… you wouldn't be prying. Growing up, it wasn't exactly the healthiest environment for me. My dad tried to make ends meet while my mom… well, she chose to drink. To go out. It took a toll on me and my dad and slowly broke us apart as a family. She sometimes reaches out, but mostly she just drank and chased men. Very unstable."

I nod slowly. "That must have been really tough."

"It was. I had to grow up fast for my little sister."

I raise an eyebrow. "You have a little sister?"

He nods, gazing out at the lunchtime traffic. "Callie. Not so little anymore. Maybe I should message her... she wanted to escape our family's chaos, so she moved away. Total free spirit."

I watch Penny approach, two steaming coffees in hand. "You should message her, see what she's been up to. I wish I had a sibling. My mom figured out pretty quick that having a kid meant it couldn't be all about her anymore, so she decided one was enough... maybe even too much."

"Siblings are bittersweet," Ryan smirks.

"Here are your coffees," Penny chirps, placing the black coffee in front of me. I roll my eyes at the simple orders, her notepad, and the fact she still manages to mess up.

Ryan switches the cups with me as Penny laughs loudly, "Oh, silly me! Shouldn't have stayed up so late last night."

She skips away, and I groan. I'm slowly starting to dislike this younger generation. I'm not that much older, but being called 'ma'am' definitely has its downsides.

Ryan blows on his coffee, looking like a walking caffeine commercial. I do the same as I hear him ask, "So... if you don't mind me prying a bit, what's really going on with your marriage?"

Bold. Like his coffee.

"I was in love with Greg once—don't get me wrong. He gave me those cliché butterflies and the constant need to be near him. But a little after we got engaged, something changed. Or maybe... the issues we had never went away. He... well, he drinks. More than I like."

Ryan nods slowly. I usually keep my guard up, especially about my problems. But something about Ryan makes me think he can understand—even if he hasn't lived it himself.

"Alcoholism's no joke," he says. "It's like any other addiction. It's not as easy as dropping the bottle and walking away all chipper. It takes real work, dedication. Has he tried getting help?"

I snort, taking a sip of my coffee to stall. Instant regret—the burn stings my tongue as the coffee's still way too hot. "He said he's been going to AA meetings, but… if he was, it lasted about two weeks. Now whenever I bring it up, he just argues. I guess I just… deal with it."

Ryan leans in, eyes serious. "For someone whose job is giving love advice, you seem pretty lost in your own love life, Fran. If you're not happy, you're not happy. And if he doesn't want to change, well… he doesn't want to change. It's that simple. You owe yourself one real conversation with him. If he still refuses to work on himself—for you, for the relationship—then you need to seriously weigh your options."

My heart hammers in my chest. "I know. It's just… scary. My family will ridicule me."

Ryan shakes his head, "The last thing I'd guess is that you let your happiness depend on your family or anyone else. Think about you—what makes *you* happy."

**You. You do.**

I glance down at my engagement ring, sparkling like it's mocking me. I brave another sip—this time cooler. "It's also the money we already put down."

Ryan bursts out laughing, shaking his head. "Using money as an excuse to stay in a relationship? That's awful, Fran. It's *money*. We're talking about your *happiness*."

How does he always know just how to shut down my ridiculous excuses? Is it his job? Or does he just get me?

I try to joke, lightening the mood, "Let's be honest—you just want me all to yourself."

Ryan's smirk grows into a full-on grin, dimples and all. "Caught me. You're sharp. But seriously—sit down with your fiancé, Fran. For you."

I feel a flicker of resolve spark inside, courage swelling like a tide ready to crash. Maybe tonight's the night I finally figure this out.

"That was some good coffee. Thanks for showing me this place," Ryan says, standing.

I rise, Penny waving her lively curls as we step outside. "Anytime. It's perfect for lunch breaks—close by and plenty of good options."

Ryan places a hand on my arm, warm and steady. "Good luck tonight, Fran. Sometimes, you have to be selfish."

I hug him, then turn back to the studio for a little more airtime.

*Ah, pride. One of the best kinds*, the figurine's voice whispers in my mind from home. **You should listen to that hunk of man, Franny. Be selfish, be prideful. It just might make you happy again.**

I stare ahead, the city buzzing around me, the figurine's words lingering like a secret challenge. Maybe it's time to figure out exactly what's going on with that antique I bought.

# Four

I smell it before I even open the door—the heavy, stale scent of beer hanging in the air like it pays rent. The living room is alive with the sounds of a hockey game—cheering fans, clashing sticks, and another goal that ties the score.

"Yeah, get 'em!" Greg's slurred voice cheers from inside. I cringe as I drop my purse on the table by the front door.

I remember when we used to watch games together. He'd gone two whole weeks without drinking back then, attending AA meetings and holding my hand like we still had a future. It felt like maybe—just maybe—we could be saved.

He turns toward me now with a drunken smirk, and just like that, the hope crashes. This is it. Time to stand up for myself—before I end up married to a man I no longer recognize.

"Franny-bear, come over here, you sexy thing."

I would rather scrape my tongue with a cheese grater... okay, maybe not.

I walk over and stop in front of him, arms crossed. He looks up at me, squinting like he's just realizing I exist.

"How was your day?" he asks, then lets out a thunderous burp.

"Very enlightening," I reply.

"Enlightening, eh?" His brow lifts, though it's clear he hasn't got a clue what I mean. "How so?"

Should I even be honest? He won't remember any of this in the morning. But before I can decide, he jabs a finger into my chest—hard.

"Ow, Greg. You wouldn't believe the day I had." I inhale slowly.

"Remember that man I met at my mother's wedding?"

He snorts. "Which one?" He grins at his own joke.

"The one who clearly made you uncomfortable," I say, and his smirk falters. His eyes sharpen—momentarily sober.

"What about him?" His tone shifts—hard now. Cold.

"He was today's guest on the show," I say cautiously. "I didn't know until he walked in."

Greg's whole body tenses, his posture rigid as stone.

"Fran, do you think I'm stupid?"

"What?"

He faces me fully now, and something in his gaze makes my skin crawl.

"I said, do you think I'm stupid? That I wouldn't see what's going on? He flirted with you right in front of me, and now he just happens to show up at your job? That's not coincidence—that's stalking."

He reaches for a half-empty beer on the glass coffee table. I instinctively put my hand on his arm.

"Greg, I'm serious. I didn't know he was a therapist. A popular one, apparently." I motion to the beer he's gripping. "But this? This has to stop."

He rolls his eyes. "This shit again? Fran, I try."

I let out a bitter laugh and pull my hand away. "You try? That's rich. Two weeks of AA does not make you sober. Drinking almost every day since? That's not effort, Greg. That's surrender."

"Then don't be with me," he snaps, downing the beer in one angry gulp.

I freeze.

The bottle lands with a bang on the table, and for a moment, we both just stare at it. I can see it in his eyes—he regrets what he said. He knows the weight of it. The cost.

I just don't care.

"Fine," I say, my voice low and steady. "I'm done."

Greg turns toward me, sobering fast. "Wait… I'm just—I'm drunk. I'm not thinking straight."

I step back, out of reach from his fumbling hands. "No. This is it, Greg. You've made your choice." My voice hardens. "All I see in front of me is a disappointment. A pathetic excuse for the man I used to love. This is *my* house. I expect you to be out by Sunday."

He shoots to his feet with alarming speed. "Don't be stupid! You need me! We love each other!"

I shake my head, the tears pricking, but I hold them back. "This isn't love. Stop lying to yourself."

"We're... we're getting married!"

"Not anymore."

I grab my coat and reach for the figurine on the shelf. Greg stumbles over the ottoman, reaching for me, desperate now.

"Please, Fran," he begs. "I'll stop drinking. I swear. For good."

I don't flinch. I don't look back.

"Goodbye, Greg."

I place the engagement ring gently on the table by the front door, then close it behind me. His cries are muffled instantly. All that's left is the strange, airy lightness swelling in my chest— the kind that only comes from finally doing what you *should* have done a long time ago.

Pride.

**Hell yes, honey. Feel the pride. Doesn't it feel so good knowing what you deserve, finally?**

I blink. That damn figurine again.

I climb into my car, hands shaking as I buckle up. I dig her out of my purse. She's glowing. *Again.*

"You. What is this? What... are you?"

Silence.

"Oh, now you're quiet? You sure had a lot to say when I couldn't talk back."

**Trust my process, lovely. Let's just say I'm your guardian angel and leave it at that for now. Since acquiring me, you've met someone wholesome, someone worthy of you. You also removed someone toxic, untrue to your soul. Trust the process and enjoy the ride. At the end, you'll thank me.**

I stare at her. What the hell am I supposed to say to that?

"I... your process? Look, I'm going to the store I got you from. Maybe the woman there can explain what kind of cursed Etsy item you are."

No reply. The glow fades, and she's just carved wood again—mockingly lifeless. I sigh and shove her back in my purse, next to gum wrappers and rogue Q-tips. *Maybe she deserves something cleaner.*

I start driving, but not toward the store. A quick Google search told me it's closed for the weekend. How convenient.

I bite my lip, and the sharp taste of blood fills my mouth. At a red light, I fumble for lip balm and smear it across my bottom lip like armor against my own nervous habits.

Eventually, I pull into a hotel parking lot. I don't know if I'm ready to check in—or if I should call someone. But definitely not my mother—she's off enjoying yet another honeymoon with husband number... what are we on now? Five?

I consider Betty. She might let me stay with her. Then I picture her and Phil, all cuddled up in their love bubble, and—no thanks. I'd rather spoon with a public park bench.

*Hotel it is.*

I feel the vibration in my purse before I even unzip it.

Greg's name lights up the screen in big white letters.

*In your dreams, buddy.*

I shove the phone back in my bag, silencing the buzzing guilt that's trying to crawl back in. The vibration dies as I walk into the hotel, the wind from the automatic doors tousling my hair like I'm starring in a very dramatic indie film.

Behind the front desk stands a woman with bright coral lipstick—some of which has migrated onto her chin—who beams at me like I'm not halfway to a nervous breakdown.

"Hello, miss! Thank you for choosing Days Inn for your stay!"

I mumble my info, swipe my card, and within minutes I'm pushing into a room that smells like recycled air and faint lemon cleaner. The kind of room that's too clean and too sterile to feel like anywhere, but perfect for not being *home*.

Why don't these windows open? Do they *want* their guests to suffocate in existential dread?

My phone buzzes again—Greg. Again. Unrelenting, like guilt in a cheap tuxedo.

I power it off.

I collapse onto the bed, the pillow firm like a lecture from a high school guidance counselor. I dig into my purse and pull out the figurine. She stares back at me—sultry, silent, smug. The intricate details, the polished wood, that unnatural little smirk.

*Guardian angel,* she claims. Guiding me through some vague "process."

Since buying her, I've met Ryan. Left Greg. Made decisions I'd been too scared to even *consider* before. Coincidence? Curse? Cosmic kick in the pants?

How does a carved piece of wood have the power to reroute a life?

I stare at her until my eyes begin to droop. Eventually, sleep creeps in, heavy and welcome. The figurine slips from my hand and lands beside me, unmoving. Mute. Mysterious.

But even in sleep, the questions echo louder than dreams.

# FIVE

The AC whirs to life, dragging me out of sleep. My eyes flutter open to the unfamiliar beige walls and bleached sheets of the hotel room I checked into last night. I reach for the nightstand on my left and power on my phone.

18 missed calls. 15 text messages.

All from Greg. Of course. What did he expect? People who refuse to change always seem the most shocked when someone finally walks away. I can already hear his voice in my head: *"How dare you!"* or *"We're about to get married, Fran—have some respect!"*

Greg's the type of man who inherited the "I'm-never-wrong" gene. He doesn't understand ownership. Doesn't grasp how his toxic traits ripple out and bruise everything in their path. I'm tired of being collateral damage.

My phone buzzes again. His name flashes across the screen. I bet he didn't sleep—probably spent the night drinking and staring at the front door like it might apologize for me.

I slide to answer, exhaling through my nose. "Hello?"

The antique store is open now, and I've got bigger questions than Greg's recycled pleas.

"Francine, holy shit, what the fuck?!"

"Greg. What do you want?" I ask, walking toward the bathroom, every syllable laced with exhaustion.

"I want to know that you're safe! I was worried out of my mind!"

I shrug. "I'm fine."

"Last night wasn't you. You didn't mean it. I swear, I'll stop drinking. For real this time."

"Enough," I snap. "I'm done. Please have all your things out by Sunday."

I hang up before his angry protests can crawl through the speaker. My heart hammers like it's afraid of the silence, but I keep breathing. I remind myself: *No more drunken stupors. No more broken promises. No more excuses.* I am free.

I wash up, check out of the hotel, and wonder what I'll do with myself until Sunday.

Driving into Dudsville, the graffiti-covered welcome sign greets me like an old joke. I pass the same rows of crooked shops and faded awnings until I spot the familiar antique store. I grip the wheel, then my purse, feeling for the carved figure inside.

The bell jingles as I step through the door.

No beads part this time. Instead, an older man with a kind smile greets me. "Hello, little lady. What can I do for you?"

"I... I bought this a little while ago—from an older woman who works here," I say, pulling the figurine from my bag.

He chuckles and shakes his head. "Oh boy. Here we go again."

"What?"

He starts dusting off a nearby lamp with a cloth, shaking his head with a half-smile. "Samantha sells that thing all the time. Every time, it winds up right back here. No idea why it won't stay gone."

My brow furrows. "She told me she just got it in."

The man laughs, soft but knowing. "That's her favorite line. Makes it sound rare. You here to return it?"

I shake my head. "No. I actually wanted to talk to her about it. It's… raised a lot of questions."

"She's home today. Not feeling too well. I'm her husband, filling in."

**You can thank me for that relationship.**

I raise an eyebrow at the figurine's unsolicited commentary and nod at the man. "Okay. I'll come back another time."

"Sorry, miss," he says with a shrug.

I nod in understanding, my eyes skimming the antiques nearest the door. Nothing calls to me—good. I'm not about to buy anything else from this place until I figure out what this little wooden mystery really is. One magical antique is more than enough, thank you very much.

Back in my car, I turn the ignition and the radio flickers to life mid-song. The Beatles. Of course. A memory barrels in like a freight train: an early road trip with Greg, just after we met. This song had played through his beat-up old speakers, each bass note making the car shudder. He danced like a madman behind the wheel, making me laugh so hard I couldn't breathe—half in joy, half in sheer terror because he wasn't watching the damn road.

I blink, returning to the present. The song has already ended, and my car's Bluetooth is lighting up with an incoming call. My mother.

Let me guess. She's getting divorced again? Realized over a plate of beachside shrimp cocktails that husband number *whatever* isn't the one either?

I tap to answer. "Hello?"

"Francine Anne Goodwin!"

I flinch, her voice loud and grating—vintage Mom. "Holy... what, Mother?"

"Don't 'what' me! You know *exactly* what you've done. Greg is in *shambles*! He didn't know who else to call. What's this about you leaving him and kicking him out?"

Deep breath. "Greg's drinking hasn't gotten better. It's hurting me—hurting us. I gave him time. I gave him *so many* chances. This was his choice, not mine."

"You would've been so well off with him, Francine. You can't possibly think your silly little talk show is enough to keep you afloat on your own?"

"S-silly?" I sputter, heat rising in my cheeks. "You want to talk silly? *Silly* is marrying an alcoholic. *Silly* is getting married twenty-five times in one lifetime. Silly is sacrificing my worth, my dreams, just to make someone else comfortable. I'm sorry you can't see that."

My finger hits the big red *End Call* button before she can reply. The silence is immediate and jarring. I stare blankly at the hotel building ahead, jaw clenched. My mother—*my mother*—caring more about Greg and being 'well off' than my happiness? Than my health?

**Yikes. That was rough. Isn't your mom supposed to be your #1 fan? Anyway, I have an idea. Let's head to that new casino down the road. Get up to a little Greed. I promise it'll be worth your while.**

I glance down at my purse, lips twitching. "Casino? Seriously? Greed? I'm not exactly in the mood to lose all my money tonight."

***Not with me, you won't.***

Oh, great. The seductress of cedar strikes again.

As the radio softly replays the final bars of the Beatles tune, I let myself smile—just a little. That road trip memory? It belongs in the *In Another Life* folder now. I file it away and pull out of the parking lot, headed somewhere I didn't expect to be today: a casino.

I weave around a black Hummer and a beige Toyota Corolla—each one likely harboring a picture-perfect family within its belly. I grimace. Why couldn't I have that? Why couldn't Greg and I have just been *normal*? A wedding that actually happened. Kids following after, like clockwork.

I stare at the painted lines slicing the road, each one ticking by like a second on a clock, carrying me closer to the casino. The building comes into view, pulsing with the energy of hopeful gamblers. I park and step out, pausing just long enough to ask myself why on earth the figurine thinks *now* is the time to go gambling.

But then I picture my house. I picture Greg maybe still being there.

Nope. Casino it is.

"ID?"

I blink and turn to my left, blushing slightly. She's asking *me* for ID? That's new. I hand over my license with a small smile. She gives a nod and jerks her head toward the entrance.

Inside, I'm swallowed by the sensory rush—poker chips clattering, cards shuffling, the mechanical hymn of slot machines humming through the air like hypnotic static. I head for a slot machine to ease in slowly, watching the digital reels spin.

"Hey, Sin Woman, maybe you can direct me to the winner?" I whisper to my purse like a lunatic.

No response. Of course not.

My gaze drifts across the room to one of the blackjack tables, where a small crowd is growing rowdy. Despite myself, a memory flickers to life.

---

*"Shouldn't we be working together?" I ask, rolling my eyes as Greg grins mischievously from across the blackjack table.*

*"Why work together," he says, "when beating you is so much more entertaining?"*

*"I just didn't want to embarrass you in front of all these lovely people."*

*The couple beside us giggles, and I glance down at my cards—7 and 4. Eleven. I peek up to see Greg scratching his chin like he's solving a riddle. That grin still on his face.*

*The dealer, a constellation of pimples across his cheeks, nods at me. "Hit?"*

*"Hit."*

*I turn my card. Nine.*

*Twenty.*

*"In your face, Greg," I murmur, trying not to gloat too hard.*

*He's sweating. Seriously sweating. I burst into laughter.*

*"Show your cards, players," the dealer says.*

*One by one, cards flip. Faces drop.*

*The dealer nods. "This lovely lady has won!"*

*Greg leans in to hug me. "Way to completely kick my ass."*

*"What do I get as the victor?"*

*"Follow me and I'll show you."*

*We head outside. He presses me against the car, his mouth traveling down my neck, making me shiver.*

---

I blink the memory away, feet still moving toward the same kind of table. That's going to happen for a while, isn't it? Random Greg memories triggered by iced tea, monkeys, wine decanters... This is why I never liked relationships much. There's too much pain when it ends. Too much healing that no one warns you about.

I sink into a plush chair and start playing. I lose the first round. Then the second.

Third time's the charm, right?

**Play this round. Trust me.**

I shrug, listening to the possessed antique, and play a third round.

This one feels different. As I hold my cards, the pot catches my eye. That's a *large* pot. The other players glance around anxiously, hoping it's theirs.

Dealer calls, "Show your cards."

Yep. I won.

They glare as I nod politely, thanking the dealer before walking to the cash-out counter. Chips clink across the table, exchanged for a thick stack of cash.

Now, time for the slot machine with the half-naked woman and the monkey.

I pause, confused for a moment, then spot the design atop the machine—an exotic woman, a small blue number, and a happy monkey dancing beside her. Monkeys. Greg. Ugh.

I slide onto the stool and feed a quarter into the slot. My heartbeat quickens as the potential jackpot flashes—$300,000. Am I about to win that much? Is this cheating?

I pull the lever. The three columns spin, blur, then slow. My lip tenses—bite marks start forming.

Seven. Seven. Seven.

The machine lights up like a Christmas tree, blaring its victory tune and summoning attendants to the "naked woman" machine.

Heads turn, gasps and claps erupt around me. I flush.

An employee jogs over, joining the applause. "Congratulations, my dear!" She scans the payout, raising an eyebrow. "Looks like you've got some decisions to make. Follow me."

I trail behind her in a daze, still not quite believing this actually happened. After signing a mountain of paperwork, I walk back outside, clutching my winnings.

Holy shit. I'm rich.

Well... not a millionaire yet. But still. That's a lot of zeroes.

I slide into my car, stacking the cash on the passenger seat. Grip the steering wheel. Maybe time to go home. Definitely time for a shower.

Back on the road, now $300,000 richer, I recognize the familiar streets leading to my place.

My heart quickens. If Greg's still there, this won't be pretty.

I check my phone as I pull into the driveway—no missed calls, no texts from him. No car in sight. Good sign.

Slowly, I unlock the door and crack it open.

"H-hello?"

No answer.

I drop my purse on the table to the right. The air feels different—emptier, colder, less love. Not that the house has felt loving in a long time. Maybe it's just memories.

A faint scent of hard liquor lingers, mixed with the ghost of vicious words.

I head to the bedroom closet. Greg's fancy shirts, pants, sweaters—gone.

He actually packed up and left.

Tears threaten, but relief wins. Relief that I won't have to have that same exhausting conversation again.

It still stings, though. After all the years, all the fights. Getting married would've been unfair to both of us.

I sit on the bed, ready to hold just one soul every night now—*mine.*

My phone rings, slicing through the quiet. I stare at the empty closet, my heart mirroring the emptiness.

It rings again.

I raise an eyebrow. What's so urgent on a Sunday afternoon?

I cross the room, passing the bundle of money I won not an hour ago.

"Hello?" I answer, opening the fridge for water. Even the few leftover beers are gone. Wow.

"Hello, love," Ryan's deep voice says on the other end.

Completely forgot about this man.

"Hey, Ryan. How are you?"

"I'm well. Actually, I'm calling to check up on you. Last time we talked, you were going through some stuff, so I just wanted to make sure you're okay."

I can't help but blush like a schoolgirl holding her first crush. "That's very sweet of you. I… well, you probably wouldn't believe me if I told you."

There's a pause—long enough to make me wonder if he hung up. Then Ryan breaks the silence with confusion. "What happened, Francine?"

I take a deep breath. "I broke up with Greg. The wedding's off. Also… I won $300,000 today."

Silence. I check my phone, worried I accidentally dropped the call. Then, finally, "I don't even know how to respond to *any* of that. Can I… come over?"

Here comes the blush again. "Sure. Give me an hour to clean up a bit."

I set the phone down where I found it and head into the pantry for cleaning supplies, stirring up a cloud of dust. Greg never understood why I kept the cleaning products next to the food. My usual answer? "Quick access when you make a mess in the kitchen." This always earned him an eye roll and an unexpected grab from behind, making me squeal.

I spray the counters with Lysol, wondering when exactly our relationship crashed. When did he start choosing alcohol over us? Duh.

Next, I move to the bathroom, scrubbing every surface until it sparkles. My hands are dry and cracked from the washing, and I laugh, knowing anyone with a shred of sense would realize homes don't usually look—or smell—this perfect on a normal day.

The lemony Lysol mixed with a cinnamon candle scent floats through the rooms, turning my place into a pleasant oasis for today. Tomorrow? Back to reality.

A few raps at the door make my heart jump. I remember the first time Greg came here for our first date—the nerves, wanting to be perfect. It's the same vibe as cleaning up now: I don't always look or smell like this on a regular day. Gotta love my sweats.

I open the door to Ryan, who's holding a bouquet of     sunflowers.

"Those can't be for me!" I joke.

"Oh, no. They're for the girl I'm visiting after you," he winks. I laugh and let him inside.

"Smells good in here. Baking something?" he asks, handing me the flowers just as I grab a crystal vase from under the sink. Why is that there? And how did I know? Greg never bought me flowers.

I need to stop thinking about Greg.

"Nope, my house just always smells like cinnamon and lemon. Yours doesn't?"

Ryan chuckles. "Can't say it does. Usually, it's more like socks and boredom."

I snort, arranging the flowers on the kitchen table, the colors coming together beautifully. "Never heard that one before. Wine?"

He shakes his head, motioning toward the couch. "Let's sit and talk."

He settles into the spot Greg always claimed—perfect view of the hockey game, beer in hand. "So… before we dive into the Greg saga, how exactly did you come into $300,000?"

I run my hands through my hair. "I left the hotel this morning and… something told me to go to the casino and have some fun."

Ryan nods knowingly. "Ah, the old gambling voice."

I glance at my purse, the antique figurine tucked inside. "Y-yeah, let's go with that."

"So… you won?"

I nod. "I did. Not sure what I'll do with it yet. Maybe get a new place—this one's starting to feel a bit stuffy with memories."

Ryan looks around, like he can see the ghosts too. "True. A fresh start would do you good. What made you finally cut the cord with Greg?"

I stare down at my chipped dark purple nail polish. "The constant drinking. The toxic choices over our relationship. I'm not spending the rest of my life with someone who can't get their priorities straight."

He scratches his chin thoughtfully. "Yeah, might seem a little hypocritical to your talk show viewers if you stick around with someone like that."

I nod softly. "I was thinking of sharing this with them—showing I go through stuff too, that my advice isn't from some perfect fairy tale. Maybe they'll relate to me more."

Ryan stares at the blank TV screen—probably never showing hockey games again in this house. I secretly hate hockey, so I keep that to myself.

"That's a great idea," he finally says. "Anything that connects you to your listeners is gold."

We sit in comfortable silence, and I debate whether to pour myself a glass of wine. Suddenly, Ryan seems to snap out of his thoughts and looks at me with something I can't quite place.

"Francine," he starts, "I think you're wonderful. The way you stand up for yourself, your independence—it's refreshing, incredible. I'm... well, very interested in pursuing you. But I want to give you space to heal first."

My fingers itch to reach out and trace his stubble—just before a full beard grows in—but I hold back. I stare into his eyes, wondering: is that lust? Love? Both?

"That means a lot, Ryan. And... you intrigue me too. I do need time to find myself again after Greg and the engagement."

He leans closer, his t-shirt riding up just enough for me to catch a glimpse of some abs. Internally, I squeak.

"Of course. I can't even imagine how you're feeling right now."

He smirks. "You're a relationship expert, can't you guess?"

Ryan kisses my cheek, and I turn, letting him kiss my lips. When was the last time I kissed someone willingly? Wanting to? I brush a brunette lock from my face as he gently pushes me back.

The rush of hormones, the fire spreading through my nerves—I lean back to see his eyes open, questioning.

"As much as I'd love to do this right now…"

He finishes for me, "…you need time."

He slides back to his side of the couch, fixing his shirt—something he really didn't need to do.

I bite my lip, my body screaming for more. Ryan laughs awkwardly. "I don't know what came over me. Sorry."

"Don't apologize. I want to explore this with you, but… let's do it when it's fair for both of us."

He nods, standing up. "Well, I should head out. I'll call you soon—maybe dinner?"

I mock gasp. "Are you asking me out on a date?"

"I am."

He plants a quick peck on my cheek and waves goodbye, leaving me spinning with confusion and clarity all at once.

# SIX

The day back to work looked like it was holding a potential thunderstorm. Dark grey clouds loomed overhead, heavy and ominous. I've never been a fan of rain or thunderstorms. My friends growing up, my boyfriends—even Greg—would always say how beautiful, tranquil, and mysterious storms were. Calm, even. I snorted at that. Calm? Thunderstorms are raw energy, ready to explode at any second. Kind of like Greg after too many drinks. Not exactly calming.

I locked the car as the rain started to fall harder, racing inside just before a lightning crack split the sky. So peaceful.

Inside the office, I sank into my red chair, feeling lighter without Greg's toxic weight but still stuck in some weird limbo. Barry came in, trudging in like he'd just survived a marathon.

Barry's usually the first one here, bursting in with his classic, "Ready to rock and roll, all you fine rockers?!" Today, he settled for what looked like some leftover coffee from the early crew, pouring it into a chipped mug.

Barry was a coffee snob—he obsessed over the perfect bean, grind, and brew. I always found it amusing. But today, he looked like he'd been hit by a truck, clutching his subpar coffee and closing his eyes like it might save him.

I stood, eyebrow raised, and approached him. "How you doing, sport?"

He shrugged, eyes still half closed. "Fantastic. You?"

"H'm. Something tells me you're not fantastic. Come on, spill."

Barry took a sip and grimaced. "Ugh, who made this?"

I smirked, knowing full well I wasn't letting him off the hook. He sighed, shaking his head. "It's… complicated."

"Complicated is my middle name. Or should be. My job's built on complicated."

Barry managed a weak smile. "Accurate, Francine. I don't want to dump my mess on you, given you've got your own chaos."

"Barry, if I didn't care, I wouldn't be pressing. Now, I've got ten minutes before air time. What's really going on?"

He glanced up, a flicker of resolve in his eyes. "Alright. So, last night was my friend's 50th. Big party, naturally. We ended up at a strip club—you know, the Busty Bunnies?"

I shook my head. "No idea, but go on."

"We're loosening up, drinks flowing, watching the show. Then the birthday guy starts hollering at this blonde on the main stage. Popular one, too." He shuddered. "Then I looked closer. And realized…"

"What?"

"She looked a hell of a lot like my daughter."

If I had a coffee, I would've spat it out in a comical arc worthy of a slow-motion replay. I try to hide my grin and deadpan, "Your daughter's a lady of the night, huh?"

Barry glares at me from under droopy eyelids, unimpressed. "Very funny, Fran. I had no idea. This was bound to happen once she moved in with her slutty mother."

I glance at the clock—airtime in less than a minute. I give Barry a pat on the shoulder. "Well, we can unpack that bombshell later. I'm sorry you found out that way. You'll get through it."

He lets out a sigh so deep I think it echoed. I leave him to his crisis and my now-forgotten quest for coffee—sweet, creamy salvation. Bitterness masked by sugar and cream. Like me. Coffee just *gets* me.

As I settle in, prepping for a parade of grief-stricken humans desperate for relationship triage, my mind wanders to Barry's situation. How *would* I feel if I had a daughter who turned to stripping? I've heard they make killer money—but at what cost? Morals? Innocence? Then again, what even *are* morals these days? I internally nod. Nope. I wouldn't be okay with it.

Of course, I don't even know if I *want* kids. But hey, imagining worst-case parenting scenarios is free therapy.

The red *ON AIR* light flickers to life, and I take a breath as Barry gives me a sluggish point from behind his mug. Showtime.

"Before I dive into helping all you lovely folks, I want to be real for a moment—show you I'm human, too. I've got problems, messy ones, just like you. Some of you already know this, but I was engaged… to an alcoholic. And the truth is—I haven't felt happy or fulfilled in a long time.

So the other day, I did the hardest thing I've ever done. I walked away. I told him I couldn't do it anymore. I need to find *my* happiness." I pause, taking a breath and catching Barry's wide-eyed stare from the corner of my vision. My cheeks flush, but I keep going.

"It wasn't easy. It was brutal, actually. But I realized I was getting married for *him*. For my *mother*. Not for me. And no matter how much you love someone—or think you do—you can't sacrifice your own peace to keep the boat floating."

I glance at my phone as it buzzes hard enough to rattle the mic stand. Greg. Of course. His name flashes in angry capital letters. I flip the screen over without another thought and breathe out slow.

"This is just a reminder that even radio relationship experts can have a full-blown romantic implosion. So if you're out there feeling stuck, scared, or unsure—remember this: follow *your* happiness. Not your mom's. Not your partner's. Yours. You get one life—as far as we know—so live it like it matters."

A beat of silence. Then, a crackle in my headset.

"–anyone there?" a girl's voice squeaks through, small and unsure.

I lean in, voice soft and warm. "Yes, love. I'm here."

"Oh, perfect. First of all, I'm so sorry you're going through a breakup," the caller says gently. "You're so strong for sharing that with all of us. It really makes us believe you're human too!"

"Aw, thank you. What's your name?"

"Beatrice. Bea for short."

"Well, Bea, what can I help you with today?"

"My... future mother-in-law is, well... controlling. My fiancé's a full-blown momma's boy. He wants to please her before *anyone* else. She's completely taken over our new home—telling us where the furniture should go, how to decorate, everything. Don't even get me started on the wedding."

Bea's tiny voice sounds exhausted, like she's been holding this in for too long. I nod at the mic, already seeing the red flags from a mile away.

"Ah, the classic monster-in-law. Have you mentioned any of this to your fiancé?"

She scoffs, "He'd absolutely take her side. So I've just... let her run the show. From where the couch goes to making the entire wedding *pink*. PINK!"

I wince. "As hard as it might be, I really think you should talk to your fiancé about this. You might be surprised by how he reacts. And even if he *does* side with her, at least your feelings are finally out in the open. That has to count for something, right?"

I can practically hear her shrug. "Yeah, I guess. Anything seems easier than actually confronting *her*."

"Well... why don't you?" I offer gently. "I mean, maybe her son marrying a confident woman would make her feel proud."

"She doesn't do well with criticism. Like, *at all*. I once saw her pick a fight with a waiter because her pasta had six tomatoes instead of eight. It was '*obvious*,' apparently. Psycho."

I stifle a laugh. "Okay, yeah, that's rough. But here's the thing, Bea—talk to your fiancé. If he's the man you're about to marry, he should want you to feel heard. If he's supportive, then the two of you can present a united front. Maybe offer the mom a small role in the wedding to help her feel included. Like planning a special dance or letting her choose the favors or something minimal. That way, she feels valued but not in control."

There's a pause before Bea says, "That actually makes sense. Thank you, Fran."

"No problem, Bea. Wishing you a love-filled day."

Click. On to the next one.

Usually, Barry would be flashing his signature goofy thumbs-up after a call like that, or at least still looking shell-shocked from my heartfelt on-air breakup bombshell. Instead, he's staring into his coffee mug like it holds all the answers—or at least the image of his daughter working a pole. I stifle another laugh as I move on to the next few callers.

And let me tell you, they don't disappoint.

By the time I finally get up for coffee, my soul feels slightly bruised. The last caller confessed he had a… fetish involving dogs. *Dogs.* I had to tread lightly, offering advice that wouldn't offend or get us kicked off air.

One of the most fascinating (and completely unhinged) parts of my job is the wild spectrum of issues people call in with—cheating, falling for a "just-a-friend," someone wanting to marry their childhood doll, and yes, dog fetishes. You think you've heard it all, then someone hits you with a curveball from left field that makes you question humanity *and* your lunch.

Still, love is love. And my job is to help people through it.

Now, finally, I get to help *myself.*

"You good?" I ask Barry, pouring myself a cup of hot coffee—finally. I watch the steam curl upward, a warm little promise of internal joy.

He doesn't answer right away, and honestly, I don't blame him. Some mornings, the weird just hits you harder.

"Yes. That was… quite brave of you, Fran. I had no idea you were going through that," Barry says, still holding his coffee like a lifeline. "You help others for a living, but I hope you take time to help yourself, too."

I nod, feeling the warm steam on my face like a mini therapy session. "Sometimes I forget. But if anyone should know how to navigate crazy love, it's me." I pause. "Oh, and Barry?"

He looks up, weary but listening.

"Talk to her. Get her side of things. I can't imagine how *I'd* feel in your shoes, but here's the thing about negative feelings—they're poison. And the only way to get rid of them is to face them. That's why I help people on a talk show. Key word: *communication.*"

I take a sip of my coffee—it's more bitter than my usual overpriced Starbucks order, but it'll do. Barry slowly rises from his chair, shoulders a little less slumped.

"You're right," he says. "I'll head to her place on my lunch break."

I smile. Another soul nudged back into connection. Just another day at the emotional ER.

Then my phone buzzes on the desk.

Greg. Of course.

Persistent little bugger.

I stare at the screen for a beat before sighing and swiping to answer. "What?"

"Francine, are you *serious?!*"

He sounds drunk.

It's 10:04 a.m.

Wow. Classy.

"I always am," I reply coolly.

"Did you just out our problems to the entire world on your *show?!* That's low. Even for you," he spits.

My eyes nearly roll out of my head. A sudden itch prickles at the back of my skull. Then a voice. *Her voice.*

**Lash out at him, honey. Show him your worth. You don't deserve this.**

Without hesitation, I step out into the hallway, shutting the door behind me like sealing off a war room.

"Listen here, you obnoxious drunkard," I say, my voice a blade, sharp and clean. "I am *done* with your pathetic attempts to glue us back together when your real soulmate is whatever's in your damn bottle. So do me a favor—stop calling, stop hoping, and stop pretending this was ever going to work. Got it?!"

Silence.

Glorious, stunned silence.

I can hear his breathing, ragged and unsure. For once, *I* have the upper hand.

I don't usually lash out. I used to bottle it up, plaster on a smile, and keep moving. But things are different now.

*Different* feels *damn good.*

"…Fran?" he finally mutters. "Who even *are* you? What happened?"

"I became someone better," I say. "Someone who knows she deserves more."

He tries one last pathetic jab. "What, did some other guy whisper this in your ear to get you to leave me?"

I smirk. "No. An antique did."

I hang up.

Just like that.

Lightness floods my chest. Joy, even. This… this is freedom. This is peace. I can already feel the weight of Greg sliding off my shoulders like a soaked coat in the sun.

I feel a smile stretch across my face—wide and real. One I haven't felt in a long, long time. I pat my bag, whispering, "Thanks, girl. Thanks."

***There's more where that came from, sweetheart,*** she purrs. ***We ain't done yet.***

# SEVEN

The day I finally got some answers was bright, warm, and unnervingly calm—like the world *knew* something was coming. As I drove down the winding country roads toward Dudsville, I tapped my index finger anxiously against the steering wheel cover.

I kept replaying the call I'd gotten just an hour earlier, my heart still buzzing from the moment I recognized the voice on the other end.

"Hi, dear. This is Samantha Hedgeway from *Granny's Treasures*."

"Hello, Samantha! How are you?"

"I'm well. I heard through the grapevine that you visited my shop a few days ago. What can I help you with?"

"I actually had a few questions about the *Woman of Sin* antique I bought from you a while back," I said, switching her to speakerphone as I tugged on a pair of ankle socks.

"Ah, yes," she hummed. "Would you like to come by? I imagine you'd prefer your questions answered face-to-face. I'll do my best."

"That would be wonderful," I said, grabbing my phone and keys. "See you soon."

"Oh, and dear?" Her voice turned serious, almost maternal. "Come with an open mind."

Now, as I roll past modest houses and vibrant graffiti murals in the heart of Dudsville, I ease off the gas for the reduced speed limit and take it all in. The street art is especially striking—bold, wild, and somehow tender. I've always admired graffiti. There's something about that rebellious artistry, the way someone can turn a spray can into a confessional. It tells stories, like scars.

Lost in thought, I almost miss the storefront. I slow, reverse, and park just under a rusted old sign warning: *No Parking Between 9–5 PM*. It's 4:50. Close enough.

The car beeps twice as I lock it. I pause outside the door, breathe deep, and step into the shop. The familiar bell jingles.

"I'll be right out!" Samantha calls from the back.

While I wait, I browse. There's a new rocking horse I haven't seen before—its mane frayed, one eye missing. Otherwise, nothing really catches my attention.

"Well, hello there." I turn around to see Samantha emerging from the back, still glowing with that odd, effortless poise. "Pleasant drive?"

"Yes, actually," I reply. "I was admiring the graffiti in your town."

She chuckles as she walks to a nearby table, brushing away imaginary dust. "Ah, I'm glad someone appreciates the hooligans' art."

I raise an eyebrow. "You don't agree with it?"

She shrugs, smiling. "I believe in expression. If art is the outlet, so be it. But it is technically city property, so…" She trails off, fingers dancing over polished wood.

I watch her float through the shop like a feather on a breeze, cleaning antiques that don't need cleaning.

"So," she says, "Francine. You mentioned questions about the *Woman of Sin*?"

I nod and reach into my purse, pulling out the figurine and placing her gently on the table between us. It almost feels rude not to handle her with reverence.

"Yes," I say. "Weird things have been happening."

Samantha's expression doesn't shift. "What kind of weird things?"

I run a thumb over the delicate carvings on the figurine—the seductive tilt of her eyes, the mischievous curve of her lips. "This is going to sound… a little unhinged. Since I brought her home, I've been hearing a voice. A woman's voice. She sounds like… I don't know, like a wise, nurturing mother figure. At first, it was scary—she was pushing me to do bold, maybe reckless things. But lately…"

I hesitate, heat rising to my cheeks. "Lately it feels like she's helping me. Protecting me. Like she *wants* me to become something better."

Samantha watches me with that same unreadable calm, then quietly says, "…like she's guiding you to your destiny."

My eyes snap up to hers, heart quickening. "Yes. And sometimes, she glows. Like… actually glows."

Samantha nods, as if I'd just confirmed something for her. "Yes. That glow—subtle, but unmistakable."

I lean forward, whispering almost conspiratorially. "Samantha... what is this antique? What did I buy?"

She smiles, not kindly, not unkindly—more like a teacher waiting to reveal the next chapter of a lesson.

She motions for me to follow her behind the beaded curtain—the one she's entered through so many times before, always with a touch of flair. The beads create their own little performance, a soft clatter like wind chimes in a slow dance as I brush them aside.

The back of the store feels like stepping into another world. Warm. Earthy. The furniture is all wood—each piece looking like it has stories to tell—except for a small, humming mini fridge in the corner. Wisps of incense trail lazily from a weathered table, wrapping the room in a scent that's somehow both spicy and sweet.

"This place is gorgeous," I say, genuinely smiling as Samantha flips the kettle on.

She glances over her shoulder. "Why, thank you, dear. We like to think of it as our little wooden getaway. Sometimes I forget I even have a home to go to!"

I laugh, easing into a creaky chair that groans a bit under my weight but doesn't protest too much. The calm here settles over me like a blanket.

"Would you like some tea?" Samantha asks. "It's a bit of a ritual when it comes to antique conversations."

"Yes, thanks," I nod, watching her move with a kind of practiced grace. She's not rushing, but she's deliberate. Everything she touches feels part of a dance she's done a thousand times.

She selects two delicate cups just as the kettle starts its whistle. The sound is high and clear—sharp enough to slice the silence. She hums softly as she pours the hot water over the tea bags, letting them steep with care. Handing me one, she asks, "Sugar or milk?"

"I'm okay," I say, eager to get to the real reason I'm here.

She sits across from me, fanning out her long skirt like royalty, and folds her hands in her lap. Her eyes gleam with something ancient—wisdom, maybe, or memory. She's waiting for *me* to start.

I clear my throat. "Like I mentioned earlier, it seems as if the figurine… talks to me. She's guided me toward choices I probably wouldn't have made on my own."

Samantha nods slowly, blowing softly on her tea. The steam coils around her face, giving her an almost ethereal glow. I watch her sip delicately, wondering how she can drink it while mine is still trying to murder the surface of my tongue.

The silence stretches thin. I feel like I'm being studied. Or tested.

Trying again, I set my cup down with a soft clink. "So because of that, I wanted to know—"

She cuts in, sharp and sudden. "Francine, dear. Have you ever wondered why she's called *The Woman of Sin*?"

I blink. "Of course. It's… quite the name. I've thought about it a lot, actually. The word *sin* definitely stands out. I assumed it had to do with her being so… sultry. Flirty, even."

Samantha lifts one eyebrow, amused. "So to you, sin equals flirting?"

I laugh, caught off guard. "No! I mean, that's just the impression I got from how she looks. That's all."

She seems to mull that over like I've just said something deeply philosophical. I am not used to this much attention on my words.

Reaching into my purse, I pull out the figurine and place her gently on the table. Her carved curves catch the light, her arms frozen in an eternal dance. She looks right at home here.

"Lust. Greed. Gluttony. Sloth. Pride. Envy. Wrath," Samantha recites, her voice a soft whisper, almost reverent.

I pause mid-sip. "I'm sorry?"

She leans back, her gaze resting on the figurine. "Those are the Seven Deadly Sins. Tell me, Francine… since you've had her, have you experienced anything that felt like committing a sin?"

I bite my lip, the thoughts bubbling up—*lust* with Ryan, *wrath* with Greg—each memory now tethered to the figurine in my purse.

"Yes," I admit softly. "Definitely."

Samantha watches me as I uncross my legs and then recross them the other way. There's something knowing in her eyes. I swallow. "So… does that make the figurine *bad*? Does it make *me* bad?"

She leans back, gaze drifting to the little wooden woman between us. That familiar, calm smile touches her lips.

"Tell me, Francine… how has your life changed since she came into it?"

I blink, caught off guard by the question. "Well… very different," I say, laughing nervously. "I broke off my engagement with someone who made me miserable. I met someone new—someone who actually sees me. I gambled for the first time—Greg never let me do that—and I won. A lot. So… yeah. I guess things have gotten better. More exciting. More… *me*."

Samantha's smile deepens. "Exactly. That is what she's here for. To guide people—many people—toward their true potential. Their true purpose on this planet."

I stare at her, stunned. "How… how do you know all this?"

She doesn't answer. Just smiles that maddening, mysterious smile and stands, smoothing out her skirt. "Well... I should get back to work. But as your journey with her continues, more will be revealed. We'll see each other again."

The certainty in her voice sends a chill down my spine. I quickly finish my tea, though I know the shiver wasn't from the temperature.

She leads me back to the front of the store. A customer is browsing the shelves now—a woman in a jogger suit, grey hairs peeking out of a messy bun. I never even heard the door chime. That conversation must've pulled me into a different world.

Samantha nods a quiet goodbye, then turns her attention to the shopper.

I step outside into the crisp Dudsville air. My hand hovers over my car door, keys in hand, when something tugs at me. I pause. Turn my head.

The town stretches out before me. People strolling, kids playing, soft chatter drifting on the breeze. I pocket the keys and walk toward the sidewalk instead.

I pass homes with flower boxes and chipped paint, children outside the convenience store with sticky mouths and loud laughter, families at the park—swings creaking, slides squealing. The kind of town you'd call boring until you looked a little closer.

Honestly, Dudsville... might've deserved a better name. Finesville, at least.

I step into a small café. The barista has tired eyes but a big, warm smile. She hands me a latte that steams up into my nose like a comfort spell. I remember not to sip it too quickly. Good things come to those who wait.

*Exactly.*

I smirk down at my purse. *She* knows what I mean.

Back outside, I cradle the coffee carefully as two kids sprint past me, one yelling a breathless, "Sorry!" over his shoulder. I smile, surprised at the warmth blooming in my chest. I imagine kids of my own—little feet, big giggles, sticky fingers. Something I never let myself picture before. With Greg... the idea had felt suffocating. A drunk man and a crying baby while I tried to hold everything together? No thanks.

But now... I could see it. With the right man? Maybe even here.

I stop.

Across the street sits a modest house, a little set back from the road. A *For Sale* sign pokes out of the grass like a dare. A grinning realtor beams from the board, too cheerful for the weathered charm of the home.

Drawn to it, I cross the road. The house is perfect. Two big windows flank the front door, a smaller one winks from the second floor. It's off-white with stone accents, a narrow driveway curling up beside it.

I walk up—trespassing, sure—but I need to see more. Around the back is a small yard, a simple patch of green. I can almost hear kids playing. I can almost *see* a life.

*My* life.

Here.

The door clicks open, and the man from the real estate sign steps out, whistling a cheerful tune as he locks up. I jump, teetering on the edge of panic—do I hide behind the hedge? Pretend I'm checking out the soil quality? Bolt?

Before I can make a decision, he turns toward the street and catches sight of me, standing frozen like a deer who just got caught window shopping for someone else's life.

"Uh, excuse me, miss?" he calls, brows lifting just slightly.

I scramble to smile, heat rising to my cheeks like I've just been caught drawing hearts around his headshot. "S-sorry," I stammer, brushing a strand of hair behind my ear. "I saw the

*For Sale* sign and just… wanted to take a look."

He studies me for a beat, then smiles—crooked, easy, a little mischievous. The kind of smile that makes you wonder if this guy knows how good he looks without actually trying. His salt-and-pepper hair is charmingly tousled, a bit of stubble shadows his jaw, and his blue eyes are the kind that could talk you into buying a house—or selling your soul.

"Well, no harm done," he says warmly. "I'm the listing agent, actually. Walter Pearson."

He gestures to the sign behind him like a magician revealing his next trick. "I just wrapped up the last showing for today, but if you'd like a quick look inside… I can probably squeeze you in."

My eyebrows shoot up. "Really? That's really kind of you."

He shrugs, unlocking the door again with a practiced hand. "What can I say? I've got a soft spot for curious strangers with good taste in real estate."

I laugh, a little breathless, heart suddenly beating a bit too fast. Anticipation pulses in my chest, skipping alongside my thoughts.

*What am I doing?*

*Am I seriously considering moving here?*

And yet, as I follow him up the steps, the figurine warm and still in my purse, something in me says: *Yes. You are.*

# EIGHT

My love for coffee came at a young age. So did the realization that no one is obligated to carry your burdens—not even your parents. At the end of the day, you have to build your own happiness, your own success, brick by brick.

A perfect example of both points came when I was thirteen, just after my mother and I moved into a small condo with her second husband—the first man after the divorce from my father.

Technically, it was a two-bedroom, which meant we had "enough room." But the walls didn't agree. No matter where I went, one of them—my overbearing mother or my creepy stepfather—was always close by.

The balcony became my safe haven. Even when they were arguing inside, if I could sit outside and let the city air hit my face, I could almost pretend I lived in a different world.

One night, I was lying in my tiny single bed, watching the stars my projector cast on the walls. I had been begging for a double bed since I turned thirteen, but my mom always brushed it off. She was too busy spending money on new outfits and makeup to impress Evan, her latest mistake. I always suspected he was cheating anyway.

The door creaked open.

"Mom?" I whispered.

"No, dear. It's Evan."

He sat at the edge of the bed, smiling with a strange, unsettling smirk.

"I'm sorry you have to hear your mother and me fighting all the time," he said softly.

I sat up, clutching my comforter tighter around me. "It's okay. I can't imagine how hard it is being an adult with responsibilities."

He nodded slowly, then placed his hand on my leg.

"You're so understanding," he murmured. "Dare I say... beautiful, too?"

His hand started to move.

My skin crawled.

"Evan?!" my mother's voice rang out like a siren. For the first time in my life, I was relieved to hear it.

He stood up and left with a wink.

I didn't sleep that night. Or the next.

Days bled into each other. I stayed alert, scared he'd come back, that his hand would return. I didn't want to admit what had happened—not even to myself—but deep down, I knew. And that knowing turned me into a guard dog in my own home.

The lack of sleep made me desperate. I started sneaking sips of coffee from the pot Evan always brewed before leaving for work. I didn't even know what his job was. Something evil, I assumed. Probably kidnapping children and selling them to Satan himself.

A month later, my mother was crying on the couch, wiping mascara streaks down her cheeks like war paint.

"Don't get comfortable in this condo," she muttered. "It's over with Evan."

I stared at her. My chest felt like it might crack open.

"I'm glad you and Evan didn't work out," I said.

She looked up, eyes wide and red. "Excuse me?"

"He... did something bad," I whispered. "He came into my room one night and... touched me."

She turned to me slowly, calculating. You could see the war in her eyes—trying to decide which truth was easier to live with: that her daughter had been hurt, or that she had married a predator.

She chose wrong.

"Stop making up stories, Franny. We all have scary dreams sometimes. Evan was a confused soul, and it's best for all of us if he moves on. Thanks for listening, Franny."

*Thanks for listening.* Like I'd just sat through one of her pity-party rants about rent or split ends, not just dropped a truth that burned holes in my chest.

She stood up with the force of denial and continued her routine, slapping on her mascara like war paint and heading out to that greasy diner where she worked overtime for tips and trash talk.

It was Saturday, so there was no school for me. Nowhere to walk to. I brewed an entire pot of coffee and stared at it like it might answer something for me. Maybe now that Evan was gone, I could finally sleep again.

I did, eventually. But the love of coffee never left. It became my armor, my late-night lullaby. Something I could count on when I couldn't count on anyone else.

---

The first thing I notice when Pearson opens the door is the light. It floods the house from every angle, bouncing off the white walls, making the place feel clean and full of breath. Full of *possibility*.

Pearson leads me into the living room, where a long table holds a gleaming bowl of fruit. Definitely fake. But the kind of fake that says, *someone cared to make this look like home.*

He continues into the kitchen. "Recently renovated," he says, like a proud uncle showing off his niece's science project. "Ideal for someone who loves to cook or bake."

I run my fingers along the smooth granite countertops—my favorite. Cool, solid, dependable. "Beautiful," I murmur.

From there, we move through a sleek bathroom and into a sitting area tucked to the side of the main floor. The second large window I'd seen from outside bathes the room in light. Books line the walls, every genre you could name. I can't tell if the previous owner was a passionate reader or if this was just another staging trick, like the fruit. But it works. It makes me feel something.

Upstairs, the air shifts. There's a cinnamon smell—faint, warm, nostalgic. A candle flickers on a hallway table. I want to follow the scent like a trail to a version of me that gets to live here.

Pearson opens the master bedroom door with flair. "And *this*," he announces, "is where the magic happens!"

I roll my eyes. "Right. Super original."

He grins. "What do you think so far? Still a few more rooms."

"I'm loving it," I say. And I mean it. I can see myself here. Walking these halls. Living these days. Using these rooms.

Pearson nods, his eyes twinkling with the scent of commission. "You've got competition. Another couple's interested, but they needed time to think. Don't wait too long."

We finish the tour. Another bathroom. A guest room. Then…the small one. The window I'd noticed earlier.

It's quiet. Peaceful. A perfect space for a home office…or maybe something else.

A nursery.

Pearson locks the door behind me. "Last stop: backyard!"

We stroll around the perimeter of the house, my imagination running wild—patio set strung with fairy lights, maybe even a small pool. Summer nights with friends. Holidays with family. My heart swells like it's trying to escape my chest.

"That's it, love. Here's my card," he says, slipping a sleek black rectangle into my hand. His grinning face beams up at me from it—just like the one on the For Sale sign.

"Thanks for taking the time to check out this beauty. Give me a call! But remember, you've got competition."

I smile. "I want it."

He laughs, light and dismissive. "Sleep on it, yeah?"

I pause. Then nod. "Expect my call. I'm serious."

Pearson escorts me back to the street and waves me off with a wink. I float back to my car, giddy. I actually almost call Greg to tell him the news—like some part of my muscle memory hasn't caught up with reality yet.

But then I stop. Who do I call now?

I toss my purse on the passenger seat, the card tucked safely inside, and lean back, letting the weight of it all settle in.

*Is this the right thing to do?*

Yes.

Just one word. A quiet hum in my mind, like a note struck from the figurine itself. Affirming what I already knew. Still—an opinion from an ancient artifact doesn't hurt.

The drive home is quiet. Peaceful. When I pull into the driveway, my phone lights up again and again—texts from Ryan and Betty. I guess I've been off the grid long enough for people to notice. I park and glance at my house. It looks dim and...unloved. Like it already knows it's getting replaced with something brighter. Something better.

I exhale slowly and grab my phone.

*I'm good. May have just bought a house!*

Sent to both. The blue bubbles fly off with a strange thrill. My purse lands in a heap inside the doorway as I make my way to the over-used leather couch. It groans under me like always.

Replies come quickly. Ryan sends a shocked-face emoji that feels charmingly out of date. Betty blasts me with laughter and reminds me that dress shopping is next weekend, and I *have* to be there.

I groan, letting my head fall back. The *last* thing I feel like doing is celebrating marriage—a glittery trap with insecurity gift-wrapped in tulle. But I send her a quick:

*I'll be there. Wouldn't miss it.*

Almost instantly, Ryan calls.

I answer. "Hello, Mrs. Spontaneous!" His voice rumbles with laughter on the other end.

"That's me. How've you been?"

"Ah, you know—same old. I realized today I'm *way* overdue for a vacation. I think it's been, what... five years since I left the city?"

I laugh softly. "I think it's been ten for me."

He gasps, dramatic. "Yikes. So we're *both* overdue. Also overdue to get away from... well, an ex."

My throat tightens. Dry mouth, sudden nerves. *An ex?*

Not mine, of course. But I'd be lying if I said I didn't feel something. Hope. Interest. Something dangerously close to longing.

I try to sound casual. "O-oh, that's brutal. I swear, once we hit a certain age, people should just mature and stay exes."

Ryan laughs. "I couldn't agree more."

A beat of silence lingers. I bite my lip. Screw it—I'm curious.

"Is... she trying to get back with you?"

"She reached out," he admits, "wanted to meet up for coffee. I declined. I mean, let's be honest—exes don't just pop back in after four years for *a cup of coffee*."

My cheeks flush hot. *Jealousy?* I've never really been the type.

When Nadia Williams ruled high school with her expensive purses and magnetic charm, I turned the other way. When my two-month boyfriend got caught drooling over her in math class,

I let him go without a second thought. He tried crawling back after she rejected him in the cafeteria. I didn't care.

But Ryan?

I care.

"Yes," I say, trying not to let it leak into my voice, "definitely not just for coffee. I'm... glad you declined."

"Oh *are* you?" he teases, his voice low and playful.

I roll my eyes, even though he can't see it.

**Show him he's yours. Use that envy. Claim him. You should be next—maybe even the last—in his bed. Not some dumb ex. She had her run.**

The figurine's voice again. Calm, commanding, with just enough bite to make my pulse skip.

I chuckle—just a little. Ryan takes it as a response to his flirtation.

"Anyway," he says, "I just wanted to check in. Let me know when you're free to hang out. And hey—don't hesitate to ask if you need help moving into your new humble abode."

"Thank you. That's really kind." I pause, then add, "Ryan?"

"H'm?"

"I'm... very interested in you. Remember that."

The silence that follows is warm. Charged. I can hear his smile through the phone.

"I'm glad to hear it."

# NINE

I feel a strong hand clasp my shoulder as I stare at the house before me. I turn halfway—Ryan's standing there, taking it in too. We fall into silence, both catching our breath from hauling an unnecessary amount of my belongings inside. Honestly, I own *so much shit* I don't even need. Exhausting. I hate moving.

He kneels beside me and grabs two water bottles from the cooler. "Here you go, new homeowner. How you feeling?"

I sigh, wiping the sweat off my brow before accepting the bottle. "Other than exhausted and currently stewing in my own sweat? Pretty damn good. Starting new somewhere... feels incredible."

Ryan places a hand on the small of my back—warm, grounding. Then, dramatically, he recoils in mock horror. "Oh, right. You *are* stewing. It's like a sauna with a personality."

I smirk and nudge him. The movers lumber past us with my king-sized bed, sweat dripping down their temples. Glancing back at the truck, I spot the last few pieces waiting for their grand entrance. A few antiques. One chair I probably should've thrown out in 2018. Almost done.

I catch myself smiling. Not at the chair. At the image in my head: me and Ryan, feet propped up in the backyard, sipping lemonade, sun kissing our cheeks.

Ryan catches me. "So you going to keep grinning like an idiot about whatever's going on in that overactive brain of yours, or are you going to help finish this move?"

I groan dramatically. My body is begging for early retirement. "I *was* imagining relaxing in the backyard. Is that a crime?"

"I think we're *all* fantasizing about relaxing right now," he says, hoisting a suitcase full of toiletries like it's a gym bag. He heads up the stairs again.

I follow with a small hallway table I'm irrationally excited about. It slides perfectly under the window like it was *meant* to live there. Interior design: nailed.

Ryan reappears from the bedroom, probably having Tetris-ed the mattress into place. He walks up behind me and presses a kiss to the back of my neck, a direct hit thanks to my mid-high ponytail.

I shriek. "I'm *so* sweaty!"

He laughs into my skin. "We've already established that, my dear." He takes my hand and leads me down the stairs, past the kitchen, and out the back door.

To my relief, the previous owners left the patio furniture behind. We sink into the cushions, the sun warm, the breeze soft. He watches me for a moment—curious, affectionate.

I tilt my head, smirking. "Like what you see?"

"Very much so," he replies smoothly, and my cheeks betray me with a blush.

He glances toward the treeline bordering the yard, then back to me. "But I was also thinking about something else... remember when I said I needed a vacation?"

"I do," I say. "And I mentioned I did, too."

He nods. "So... would you be interested in taking a trip with me?"

My heart skips. Vacation? With him? That's... soon. We're not *official*, and yet—this feels right. Still, my overthinking brain decides to clock in late.

Do couples do that so early? What about work? Can I just *go*?

**Go, Francine. There shouldn't be rules when it comes to the heart. Work can survive without you—you said it yourself. Ten years! Go be a sloth in the sun for a week. Drink fruity things with umbrellas. Maybe see him shirtless. You earned this. Have I steered you wrong yet?**

I grin. Nope. She hasn't.

"Uh, Francine?" Ryan's voice pulls me back as I stare ahead, lost in the figurine's silent encouragement. I blink, shaking myself free. "Sorry, Ryan. I was just thinking about having to request time off work and—"

He cuts me off, raising his left hand like a traffic cop. "Francine, all these excuses are exactly why you haven't gone anywhere in ten years. Don't you think you deserve a break?"

I exhale slowly. He's right. The figurine was right. "You don't think... it's too fast for us?"

Ryan laughs, deep and sure. "Not at all. Think of it as us getting to know each other better—just with nicer scenery and better drinks. What's the harm?"

"None," I admit, smiling. "Alright then. Where are we headed?"

He stands, stretching, and I catch a glimpse of abs beneath his shirt. I bite my lip. Motioning toward the front of the house, he says, "Looks like the movers are wrapping up. Let's find a café nearby and plan our escape."

I nod, excitement fluttering in my chest as we walk to the front yard. Ryan calls out, "Hey, you guys done?"

Ron, the leader of the movers, jogs over. "Yep. Everything's inside and in its rightful place. Thanks for choosing us!"

We smile and wave as the movers down their water bottles and climb into the truck, engines rumbling to life. "Thank God for movers," I say, feeling the weight of the day start to lift.

"Right?" Ryan grins, leading me to his car. "Go lock up your place. Let's find some food and plot our getaway."

---

Something Greg and I always did when we first started dating was hop in the car—usually his—and drive until we found some quirky new spot to eat. That's how we stumbled on The Cantina, a tiny Mexican joint with killer food and even better staff. I loved Mexican food like it was a genre of music—different flavors, different vibes. Greg used to tease me, "Fran, genres are for music, not food." I'd shoot back, "Different types of music, different types of food. Same difference."

"This looks like a good spot to stop," Ryan says, signaling right and snagging one of the last parking spots on the narrow street. He parallel parks like a pro. "Wow, impressive skills."

He winks, popping the car into park and undoing his seatbelt. I follow suit, and we start strolling down the street. The antique shop comes into view, bright and inviting.

"You know all those antiques I have?"

Ryan glances at me, distracted by the search for a restaurant. "Yeah, you love them."

"Well, most of them came from here." I point to the shop. Ryan peers inside, admiring the knickknacks while I watch Samantha, the owner, nodding and placing a gentle hand on a customer's shoulder.

I feel a warm familiarity as we pass. Ryan says, "Looks like a really cute place, Francine."

"It is," I say softly, remembering the cozy back room that always felt like home.

Ryan stops outside a small bistro and turns to me. "So, you're friends with the owner?"

I hesitate—there's more to it than friendship. Something I'm not sure I'm ready to share yet.

"How's this place?" he asks, smiling.

I nod and we step inside, quickly settling into a cozy booth near a side window. No debate — booths are the best. Who wants to sit in a hard chair when there's a comfy, all-enveloping booth ready to hug you?

"Yeah, you could say that," I smile, answering Ryan's question. "I've been there enough times to be on friendly terms. We sat in the back, sipped some tea, and had a nice chat about antiques."

"Nice," Ryan nods, genuinely interested. "What's been your favorite antique?"

I flash a knowing smile. "A delicate, feminine figurine. She's about the size of my hand and gives off these... magical, weird vibes." That's the closest I'm getting to the truth for now. One day I'll tell Ryan about the whole 'figurine-guiding-my-life' saga, but not yet. Can't scare him off before we're truly close. Besides, I don't want to sabotage my first trip in years now that I have a partner-in-crime.

I'm independent—walking through life solo is my jam—but when it comes to travel, exploring new places, soaking in new cultures, I've always believed it's better shared. Greg?

Nah. His idea of exploring was getting drunk on local beers. His version of culture shock was just the hangover.

"Sounds intriguing," Ryan says, grabbing the plastic menu to his left. "Now, how about we figure out what this place serves and then discuss where we should go?"

"Go? Oh—on the trip!" I realize.

"Yes, the trip. I meant it," Ryan says, raising an eyebrow. I giggle, grabbing my menu as well. "Well, so did I. And honestly? I'm actually pretty excited."

Our waiter appears—a young guy with a notepad, clearly fresh on the job, nerves practically radiating off him like heat waves.

"Can I get you started with something to drink?" he asks, biting his lip.

"Yes, a coffee would be amazing," I say. Ryan nods, "Same for me!"

The kid scurries off, and I rest my chin on my left knuckle, studying Ryan.

"So... idea. Ever been to Mexico?"

Thinking of The Cantina on the way here made me dream of authentic Mexican food anytime I wanted in a beautiful place. Ryan's eyes light up.

"No, never! What made you suggest Mexico?"

"Well, it's my favorite food. Plus, it looks gorgeous. So, putting two and two together..." I trail off, cheeks warming.

Ryan chuckles and glances behind me just as two coffees arrive, one spilling a little onto the table. The kid blushes harder than I thought possible. "So sorry, sir."

"No worries. I think we're ready to order."

After we finish ordering our respective sandwiches, Ryan pulls out his phone. A flicker of irritation flashes through me — please don't be one of *those* people who scroll mindlessly through social media while talking to someone right in front of them. But then he turns the phone toward me, revealing a stunning resort glowing under the Cancun night sky.

Ah. So he *is* perfect.

"This is Temptation Resort in Cancun," he says, swiping through vibrant images of lively parties, luxury pools, and that picture-perfect beach. "What do you think?"

I can't help but feel like this place was made for me — the bright colors, the endless amenities, the gorgeous ocean waves calling my name. I nod, a spark of excitement flickering to life. "I think it's gorgeous."

We tap through the booking details, and surprise! They're running a promotion. "Is that doable?" Ryan asks, setting the phone down.

I fake a thoughtful tap on my chin, then grin, "Hmm, the colors could be a bit brighter..." I smirk. "Just kidding. It's amazing. Let's do it."

Excitement bubbles up as we dive into the booking process, barely noticing the sandwiches that arrive and are devoured at record speed — because, honestly, who wants to chew when there's Cancun planning to finalize?

Once the confirmation emails land, Ryan leans back, a proud grin spreading across his face. "Well, there you have it! We're headed to Cancun in two weeks — one week of sun, sand, and maybe a little mischief."

I clap my hands, and he chuckles. "I've never seen you this excited and lively."

I tap my tongue playfully. "I can be lively. But Mexico and its food? Yeah, they definitely help."

# TEN

"Barry, are you sure you can survive the week I'm gone?"

He waves me off, "Don't worry, Fran. I've got some guest stars lined up to keep me company. You haven't taken a proper vacation since you started here — you deserve this."

He hands me a coffee, and I smile, grateful. "Thanks, Barry. So, how's the situation with your daughter? Any progress?"

Barry's eyes widen, like he's just remembered the drama—or that he even told me in the first place. "Oh, that. Yeah, I talked to her like you suggested. At first, she stuttered and tried to deny it, saying I must've seen someone else. Then, get this—she flipped it on me and asked why I was hanging out at a strip club! Can you believe that?"

I arch an eyebrow, understanding the wild mind of a young adult only because I was one once. "Sounds about right. What happened next?"

He sighs, running his hands through his hair like he's trying to tame a tornado. "She finally caved after a few more denials and admitted she needed the money. But the reason… well, it's not something any dad wants to hear."

I lean in, feeling the weight of his worry. "What's the reason?"

Barry hesitates, as if deciding whether to trust me with the whole messy truth. Then he nods slowly. "She's saving up to help her boyfriend pay off some drug dealers. So not only did I find out she's stripping and has a boyfriend, but now she's wrapped up in something really dark."

I bite my lip, sympathy knotting in my chest. "Barry, I'm so sorry."

He shrugs, looking lost. "You're the expert here. How do I handle this?"

I gesture toward my big plush chair and settle in, waiting for my 'expert moment.' "It's tricky. Your daughter's trying to help someone she cares about in a way she thinks is right. The best thing you can do is have an honest, calm conversation with her. Don't judge or shame her. Instead, try to find out how you can support her—and help her find a way out of stripping and that dangerous situation."

Barry nods, doubt lingering in his eyes. "But what can *I* actually do?"

I smile, leaning forward a bit. "Funny you ask — I won some money on a whim at the casino the other day. Maybe I can lend you guys a hand."

Barry looks stunned. "No way, Fran. Those casinos are rigged! The fact you won is a miracle and should be celebrated. Plus, you're going on that trip. Use it for yourself."

I grin. "Thanks, Barry, but I really did win. Why don't you figure out what you need, come back to me, and we'll talk?"

He shrugs with a relieved smile. "Alright, I'll try. Thanks, Fran."

I nod as Barry heads out, leaving me to prepare for one of my last shows before I head off to beautiful, sun-soaked Mexico. I can already taste the tacos — al pastor, carnitas, barbacoa… yes please.

The red light flicks on, and I slip into my usual opener, just in case we've got some new listeners tonight. The first call comes through.

"Hello, Fran here. How can I help you today?"

"Hi, Fran," a girl's voice says — young, maybe 18 or 19. "I have a question for you."

"That's what I'm here for. Lay it on me!"

There's a deep breath, then — "My father caught me… well, stripping. I ended up having to explain why, which was super embarrassing. Listen… my boyfriends in some trouble with, like, really high-up people and I wanted to help him. What do I do?"

I stare at the microphone, jaw slightly open. My eyes dart over to Barry. I usually love a good pun — *high people*, wink wink — but this isn't the time. The irony is too thick to ignore. Barry's daughter? *Calling into the show?* Was this a cry for help… or a power move? Surely she knows this is *his* station?

"Ahem, Fran?" her voice prompts again.

Barry's face has gone ghost-white. I take a breath and lean back in. "Sorry, honey. I just have to ask you this first: Do you really think it's worth staying with someone if this is the life he's pulling you into?"

"He's not pulling me into anything — it was my choice! I love him!"

Ah, young love. I roll my eyes skyward, but soften my voice. "I get it. Love makes us do all kinds of wild things — even strip to help someone we care about. But… love should *never* cost you your safety."

"My life isn't in danger," she says — but the hesitation in her voice betrays her.

"Right," I reply gently. "Listen… maybe try talking to your dad again. I promise you — all any parent wants is to support their kid. Even if they're shocked at first, deep down, they just want to help. This situation? It's no different."

"My dad scrunched his nose at me and wouldn't even *listen*," she snaps, exasperated.

I glance at Barry. He winces. I hold his gaze as I answer, "Hearing something so heavy out of the blue would knock anyone sideways. But I guarantee if you talk to him again — really talk — he'll be more understanding. There's a solution to every problem, I promise. One that doesn't put you in harm's way."

There's a pause on the other end. I shoot Barry a sharp look — this is *his* moment to rise up.

"Okay… I'll try talking to him again," she finally says, her voice a little smaller. "I *am* scared. I don't like how I'm treated at the club."

"Then that's your sign. You don't belong there, sweetheart. You deserve safety. You deserve kindness. Start with your dad — and thank you for calling."

*Click.*

A few more calls trickle in and then it's time for a break. I stand, my stomach rumbling. Maybe there's still one of those mini sandwiches left in the fridge — though honestly, that feels like a long shot. Barry downs a bottle of water as I pass him and open the fridge. Jackpot — one sandwich remains.

"Well," I say around a bite, "that was something."

Barry sighs, dragging a hand down his face. "You think she *knows* this is my studio?"

"I mean, probably?" I shrug. "You said she's always on her phone, and you've mentioned how successful my show is like, a dozen times. I'd be surprised if she *didn't* know."

He shakes his head. "That's… unnerving."

I finish the sandwich and dust off my hands. "Hopefully, she took something away from the call. At the very least, it sets the stage for when you have the *real* conversation. The right way, this time."

Barry nods, slowly, like he's filing it all away for later. The weight of parenthood settles around his shoulders — but underneath it, I think I see the spark of hope.

Barry blushes as I continue, "It's just funny, isn't it? After all the messy, complicated situations we hear about and try to help with… we still go home and don't follow our *own* advice."

He chuckles, rubbing the back of his neck. "Hey, *you're* the advice-giver. I'm just the guy who brews the coffee and dodges emotional growth. Besides…" — his voice softens — "it's always harder when it's your own life. Knowing what to do and *doing* it? That's two different games entirely."

I nod, the truth of it sitting heavy but not unpleasant between us. "Yeah. Fair."

We part ways, Barry heading off to possibly confront the most uncomfortable heart-to-heart of his life, and me…well, I settle back into my seat with Mexico dancing across my mind. Tacos. Sun. Maybe some healing of my own.

The red light glows again. Showtime.

# ELEVEN

Airports hold a lot of possibility—love reunited, new adventure, maybe even a fresh start. I've always found comfort in watching people move through terminals, each one carrying their own story. Everyone's headed to the same destination, but for completely different reasons. Some are going to meet lovers. Some are off on honeymoons. Others might be escaping a marriage entirely. Who knows?

I've always wanted to ask every passenger how they ended up on *this* flight, on *this* day. What crossroads brought them here?

"Hurry up, would ya?"

I roll my eyes, snapped back to reality by Ryan's voice. I drag my massive suitcase behind me, my overstuffed carry-on purse perched like a queen on top of it.

"I'm coming. I have a lot of stuff, okay?"

Ryan chuckles, slowing his pace to let me catch up, his suitcase comically small next to mine. "I'll never understand you women—you bring an entire wardrobe, then wear maybe three outfits the whole time."

I laugh as we finally reach our gate. "Who knows what kind of situations could come up when you're out of the country? I'd rather be prepared than stuck buying overpriced emergency outfits. *That* would be wasteful. Really, it's just logical."

Ryan shoots me a look of mock disbelief, clearly amused, and points to two open seats. We park ourselves and our bags, preparing to wait for the next hour. He pulls out his phone.

"I just need to message a few people to let them know I'm about to take off. My mom still worries like I'm twelve."

I smile. "That's sweet."

While Ryan texts, I pull out my own phone and call my mom—because why not complete the emotional bingo card before boarding?

She answers with her usual cautious tone. "Hello, Fran?"

"Yes, Mom. How are you?"

She sighs. "As good as can be expected. Greg finally stopped calling me twenty times a day."

"Oh… I'm sorry he's doing that."

A pause. Then, "Look, Fran…" She trails off as the PA crackles overhead, announcing a final boarding call to Paris. "…Where are you?"

"I'm at the airport. Heading to Mexico for a few days—with a friend."

"Wow, that's... quite random. Anyway, I hope you stay safe. Don't let them abduct you."

I can't help but laugh. "I'll do my best. Hey—what were you going to say before?"

"Oh, right. I was just going to tell you... it might not seem like it, but I *am* proud of you. I know I seemed excited when you were settling down and maybe starting a family, but... Greg wasn't exactly stable."

My eyes widen at the sudden honesty. She continues before I can reply.

"And I'm sorry if it seemed like I wasn't there for you. I just never thought you'd *want* to settle down—you've always been so... particular. But if you're happy, then I'm happy."

I roll my eyes. *Thanks for the backhanded support, Mom.*

Still, I say, "I appreciate you saying that. Leaving Greg wasn't easy, but I knew it was the right thing before making a huge mistake."

"Well... have a good time in Mexico."

Click.

I glance over at Ryan, who's still absorbed in his phone. I nudge him. "So, how'd it go?"

He jumps slightly. "Exactly as expected. 'Be careful, look both ways, brush your teeth.' Classic Mom stuff. You?"

I shrug. "Surprisingly wholesome. She actually said she's proud of me and apologized for not showing it. Not like her at all. Maybe her new husband is a decent influence."

Ryan opens a bag of chips he snagged on the way to the gate, finally managing to tear it open. "That's great, Fran. Good to know she's coming around."

About ten minutes later, we board the plane and settle into our seats. Ryan takes the middle seat, giving me the window. I blush a little—it's a small gesture, but one that says a lot. Giving. Considerate. Probably good at back rubs.

I place my carry-on at my feet and glance over at the book Ryan pulls out of his bag. The cover is gorgeous—an abstract art piece in swirling colors.

"How do you like it so far?" I ask, nodding at the cover.

He pats the front of the book. "It's sucked me in. I'm a sucker for a good mystery."

I grin and lean back into my seat, watching the tarmac as the plane begins to taxi.

As Ryan delves into his book, I sit back and let the start of our journey wash over me. I've always found something oddly therapeutic about flying—watching people settle in, the click of seatbelts, the polite but clearly exhausted flight attendants checking rows. There's always one who gets stuck demonstrating how to survive a crash landing, and I can't help but wonder… how do they decide that? Is it rock-paper-scissors? A rotating schedule? Loser of trivia night?

"Hello passengers," the pilot's voice buzzes through the cabin. "This is your captain speaking. Thank you so much for flying with us today. Our destination is Mexico, where it's currently a sunny 25 degrees. Please make sure your seatbelts are fastened. We'll be taking off shortly."

Ryan glances up from his book and grins at me. "You ready? Excited?"

"To go somewhere exotic with an amazing guy?" I tease. "Nah."

He blushes. "Good!"

His eyes drop back to his pages. Judging by how relaxed the book is in his hands, he's already a quarter through it. I tilt my head. "Do you consider yourself good at guessing who did it?"

"Who did what?"

I nudge my chin toward his book. "If it's a whodunnit… think you're a decent armchair detective?"

Ryan considers this. "Sometimes, yeah. But I'll admit—I'm way better at guessing in movies than books. Books just have so much… *information*. All these little details in the shape of words.

Movies spoon-feed it to you in images. Not that I don't love books. It's just easier to catch visual clues."

"Couldn't agree more," I say. "Though when movies ruin a good book? Unforgivable."

He nods solemnly. "Justice for every butchered adaptation."

Then he notices my empty hands. "So, what do *you* do to pass the time on flights?"

"Same stuff, usually—reading or music. Though that was ten years ago, so who knows what 2025 Fran does now."

The plane starts taxiing, wheels gliding us toward the runway in a slow, creeping line. I feel my hands start to fidget, nerves bubbling up. Ryan notices—of course he does—and reaches out, gently lacing his fingers with mine. His touch is warm, steadying. I relax into it, heart rate leveling out as the plane picks up speed and lifts off the ground, slicing up through the clouds like a giant mechanical bird.

This is what's always fascinated me about modern travel: the miracle of it. Just a couple centuries ago, we had no idea there was a whole other world beyond the borders of our town or village. No clue about other cultures, other foods, other skies. Now, we casually book a trip to Mexico and sip wine over the Rockies.

Tragic, really. Not just the lost potential of past centuries—but that I haven't been anywhere in *ten years*.

As soon as the seatbelt sign clicks off, I dig through my carry-on and pull out a well-worn paperback. Not a mystery, unfortunately. I didn't have time to hit up Chapters before we left, so I grabbed a sappy romance I had lying around. *Yeah, yeah,* I know. Plot twist. But I'm already invested. Jessica and Travis have this slow-burn thing going on that's basically a Hallmark movie in book form, and I need to see them finally admit their feelings.

Speaking of feelings…

A line in the book about longing pulls me back to the present. I sneak a look at Ryan—his messy hair, his focused expression, the way his mouth moves slightly when he's reading something dramatic. I definitely have feelings for him. Not just because he's hot (though—bonus), but because he makes me feel like living again. He nudges me out of my cozy, curated bubble and makes everything feel significant. Like I matter.

My daydream is interrupted by the flight attendants making their way down the aisle, carts in tow.

"Oh, *yes please!*" Ryan says, clapping his hands together like a child about to get dessert.

I giggle. "You that excited for some measly nuts?"

"I heard they upgraded to pretzels," he teases.

I roll my eyes, smiling as a young, absurdly stylish flight attendant stops at our row. Her makeup is flawless. Her vibe screams "Instagram influencer moonlighting at 30,000 feet."

"Hello, loves. What can I get you?"

"A beer would be wonderful," Ryan says, accepting the cold can as she opens it with a practiced flick of her wrist.

"I'll have some wine, please."

She hands me a tiny bottle, gives us a cheerful nod, and glides away.

"Aw, no nuts yet?" Ryan pouts.

"You'll get them, love," I say, mimicking the flight attendant's saccharine tone from earlier.

Ryan raises a single brow, amused but silent. "Back to the book I go."

Okay, yeah. Jealousy? Not my best look. Honestly, not anyone's best look. I've never thought of myself as the jealous type—I always figured it was a waste of energy. You either trust someone or you don't. And if you don't? You walk. But now that I'm with someone I actually *want* a real shot with, that little gnawing feeling has taken up residence in my stomach like a petulant house guest.

**He's here with you, love. On a plane to Mexico. With you. No one else. That's thanks to me. You're worth it. Enjoy getting to know him.**

Her voice—soft and motherly—rings out from the overhead compartment. Yup, I brought her. The figurine. She's stowed away above us in my carry-on, watching over me like some kind of divine flight attendant. I mentally thank her, though a part of me wonders… how much of this is really her doing? And how much of it is *me* finally stepping up?

The plane ride stretches longer than I hoped. The initial thrill of travel is giving way to sore legs and a desperate craving for fresh air. The romance between Jessica and Travis heats up on the page, and just as they finally hook up—*hallelujah*—the pilot's voice crackles through the speakers again.

"Hello, passengers. We hope you enjoyed your flight with us today. We are slowly making our descent into Mexico, currently 25 degrees. Enjoy your stay!"

I wince as my ears start to pop. Ryan, ever the boy scout, hands me a stick of gum without even looking away from his book.

"Thanks. Ear popping is the *worst* feeling."

Ryan nods, chewing. "I mean, having your arm ripped off would probably rank worse, but hey, what do I know?"

He winks and I nudge him. "That's morbid, Ryan. *Morbid.*"

The plane lands with a soft bump, rolling along the tarmac as impatient passengers unbuckle and pop up like toast, all jostling to stand even though the doors are still very much closed.

"I'll never get that," I mutter. "Why stand just to wait longer?"

"People need to *feel* like they're moving, even when they're not," Ryan says, stretching. "Fake progress. Classic human condition."

He points up ahead. "Looks like we're moving now. Get ready!"

We join the migration. Ryan grabs my luggage from the overhead, and I do my best to navigate the narrow aisle without whacking my suitcase into a dozen knees. We thank the flight crew, stepping out into the humid corridor toward customs. Through the windows, I spot palm trees swaying lazily in the breeze.

It looks warm. It looks delicious. *Come to momma.*

We shuffle through customs, passports in hand, shifting from foot to foot like kids before recess. After clearing security, we scan the crowd outside for our transportation. That's when I spot it—a purple sign reading *Temptation*. I nudge Ryan, "Over there!"

The warm air kisses my cheeks instantly, dancing through my hair like it's been waiting just for me. We make our way to the bus, finding seats toward the back. I tap my suitcase along to the soft rhythm of the music playing through the overhead speakers while watching the workers load luggage with mechanical grace, efficient even in the heat.

Ryan suddenly grabs my hand, snapping me out of my daze. His touch still sends a thrill up my arm.

"Fran! We're here! Are you excited?"

I squeeze his hand as the bus doors close and the driver gets settled in his seat.

"More than you could ever know."

With some creaky brakes and a jolt, we were off. The drive to our resort was supposedly 22 minutes, so I leaned back, letting the buzz of excited chatter wash over me while the engine hummed and cars zipped past outside.

I glanced over at Ryan, catching him staring out the window. His eyes lit up when we caught glimpses of the ocean peeking out from behind scattered buildings.

"I can't wait to just float in that water," he sighed, clearly imagining it already.

"I'm looking forward to lying in the sun with multiple drinks in hand," I grinned.

Ryan rolled his eyes in mock disapproval. "Of course you are."

Soon, the bus pulled up to the resort. The driver parked with a practiced ease, turned to us with a friendly grin, and said, "Enjoy Mexico!"

"We plan to!" someone shouted behind us, clearly already in vacation mode.

We filed off the bus and into the thick, delicious heat again. After retrieving our bags, we entered the resort's sleek, airy foyer, the scent of citrus and sunscreen in the air. The check-in line moved slowly, and as we waited, reality caught up with me.

*Oh right. We're sharing a room. For a week. Just Ryan and me. Sleepovers—plural.*

I felt my cheeks heat up. We didn't talk about sleeping arrangements. I mean... there *were* two beds. But still.

"We're next!" Ryan nudged me forward, snapping me out of my internal spiral.

We checked in with a woman whose tan skin glowed like she lived inside a tanning bed and smiled like she got commission on joy. She handed us two room keys, and we headed to the elevator, then up to the fourth floor. Ryan slid the key into the door and turned to me with a raised brow.

"You ready?"

"Yes!" I said a little too quickly.

He opened the door, revealing a gorgeous room in soothing, muted tones. Through the sliding glass doors, we could see people meandering around the pool, tropical music pulsing from the bar, and bartenders blending fruity concoctions that made my mouth water. I watched someone get handed a frosty drink with a bright paper umbrella, and instinctively licked my lips.

"So, what's first on the list?" Ryan asked, tossing his suitcase onto one of the queen beds.

I tore my eyes away from the drinks. "We can unpack a bit, grab something cold, and check out the beach?"

"Great idea," Ryan said, already zipping open his suitcase.

I did the same with mine on the other bed, pretending not to wonder if *that* bed was going to be *mine*—as in solo—or if... well, if things might eventually change.

Before I could stew on that much longer, Ryan commented with a smirk, "How you got away with that weight is beyond me."

"Hey, I'm not *that* fat," I teased.

He snorted. "You're *definitely* not. I meant your excessively overstuffed luggage."

"Well, you never know when you'll feel like a red dress or a blue one," I defended. "So obviously, you pack both."

"Naturally," he agreed, pulling out a pair of socks. "Even though *I* usually prefer my slimming black dresses."

I rolled my eyes and lobbed a balled-up sock at him. "You'd rock it."

We unpacked in companionable silence, each claiming a drawer or two. When everything was neatly in place (or at least shoved somewhere functional), Ryan turned to me, eyebrows raised.

"Drink time?"

I nodded. "Absolutely."

We headed out, leaving the room and the suitcase behind. The figurine was still in there, tucked between layers of clothes, quiet now. She hadn't spoken to me since the flight.

I wonder what other tricks she has up her sleeve.

Wooden sleeves, of course.

# TWELVE

The days in Mexico were heavenly—gorgeous beaches, breathtaking hikes, and sunshine that seemed to wrap you in a warm hug. Ryan, I quickly learned, is the adventurous type—always eager for the next excursion. Me? I've always been proudly lazy on vacation. Plop me by the pool or beach with a mai tai and I'm golden all week.

We arrived back at the beach, a little downshore from our resort, after a catamaran tour. I could already feel the heat radiating off my skin—turns out I'd gotten seriously sun-kissed. Ryan waved me forward, and I trudged through the sand, the resort growing closer with every achy step. My legs were sore from snorkeling, and honestly, the sand was winning the war.

By the time I caught up, Ryan—looking very bronze and beautiful himself—handed me a mai tai. My man. He pulled two loungers together and collapsed into his with a contented sigh, sipping a piña colada.

"That was an incredible experience, right?" Ryan broke the silence.

I turned to look at him and noticed he was already halfway through his drink. My heart gave a nervous flutter. Fast drinking always triggers me—memories of someone who drank too fast, too often. I exhaled slowly and replied, "It was! I didn't put on enough sunscreen, though."

Ryan laughed, noticing the red tint on my skin. "It's easy to forget when you're on the water. We've got aloe vera back in the room. We'll head back soon."

I leaned into the lounger, lazily people-watching the pool area. A young couple—definitely not newlyweds, more like on their first vacation together—were nestled at the pool's edge, giggling and kissing. I wondered if Ryan and I would hook up on this trip. Maybe. Since Greg, I haven't really been into sex. But with Ryan? It might be different.

Nearby, two guys lying out pointed at a couple of girls grabbing drinks at the bar, clearly admiring more than their cocktails. I wondered if they were friends hoping to get lucky, or on a double date. People-watching always fascinates me. You can piece together little stories, make up entire lives from a few glances. Across the pool, an older couple lounged under a massive umbrella, occasionally nodding at each other like they'd been sharing silent conversations for decades.

Greg and I aren't going to grow old together anymore. That part of my story's over. But will Ryan and I?

I stood and pulled a big umbrella closer for some much-needed shade after our full day in the sun. Ryan watched me curiously.

"Too much sun?" he asked. "Why not cool off in the pool?"

"I was actually thinking of doing that... after getting a Miami Vice."

"A what now?"

I blinked. "You don't know what that is? It's only one of the most delicious drinks known to man. Half piña colada, half strawberry daiquiri."

Ryan's eyes lit up. "That sounds amazing. How have I never heard of that? Grab me one too?"

I nodded and made my way to the bar, wondering as I walked if Ryan was checking out my butt the way those other guys had been ogling earlier. I blushed. My ass wasn't as tight as theirs, but maybe it had its own charm?

I leaned against the cool bar counter, waiting for the bartender to notice me. When he finally did, he flashed a too-charming grin.

"Well, hello there. Welcome to Temptation! What can I get for you, beautiful?"

My face flushed—not that he could tell under my sunburn.

"Slow your roll there, cowboy," I said with a smirk. "Two Miami Vices, please."

"Great choice. Coming right up."

He turns away, giving me a perfect view of his back. He's fit—tanned, muscular, the kind of guy who probably thinks sunscreen is for amateurs. He turns back with a grin and hands over two chilled drinks, the rum floating in swirling clouds at the top.

"How are you liking the resort?" he asks.

"It's been an awesome stay so far. I really can't complain."

"Me neither. I get to see beautiful women in bikinis all day." He winks at me, leaning a little too far into the flirt.

I roll my eyes, "How flattering. But I'm actually here with someone. Good day."

With that, I pivot on my heel and head back to Ryan, adrenaline buzzing in my veins. I just admitted I was *with* Ryan. And weirdly? My heart, mind, and body all liked that truth.

I hand him his drink, and he nods, "Thanks!"

"No, thank *you*."

I stretch out again on the lounger, letting the shade cool my scorched skin. Ryan glances over. "For what?"

"For… coming into my life when I needed you."

Ryan shifts, turning fully toward me, reading the emotion in my voice. "Of course. You're a very interesting, unique person, Francine. I really enjoy… whatever this is."

I bite my lip. "About that. I'm sorry if things haven't been very clear."

"Not a problem," he says gently. "You just got out of an engagement. You're figuring things out. I get it, and I'll give you all the space you need."

I smile, genuinely thankful for how steady he is. "Thanks, Ryan. How about we finish these drinks and then get me that aloe vera?"

I take a long sip—the cold, boozy slush gliding down my throat like a delicious antidote to the heat. After we finish up, we head inside. Back in the room, Ryan starts digging through his suitcase, mumbling to himself.

"I swear it was in the zippered pouch—aha! There it is!"

He pulls out a big green bottle and turns to hand it to me. Our hands brush. We freeze.

We look at each other for a long, breathless moment, locked in that timeless gaze of "who's going to make the move?"

Considering he said he'd wait until I was ready... I guess that means it's me.

So I did.

I step closer and reach for his face, my fingers grazing the stubble on his jaw. I pull him toward me. Our lips meet—soft, warm, searching. His part slightly, inviting mine in. My tongue slips past, meeting his for the first time.

"Francine," he murmurs against my mouth, fingers threading through my salt-dried hair.

**Get it, girl!**

I giggle mid-kiss at the figurine's gleeful outburst, sounding like a hyped-up best friend watching from the dance floor.

Ryan guides us to the bed, and we fall back into it, the soft sheets cushioning us. My sunburn protests for a second, but then his hand moves down my body, and suddenly—pain? What pain?

I forget everything but this. Him. *Us.*

My body shivers in ecstasy as we become one. I dig my nails into his back, waves of pleasure crashing through every fiber, every nerve ending. Eyes closed, I let myself believe this moment—*us*—is perfect.

Ryan looks at me with pure adoration, and I meet his gaze, pulling him in for another kiss, deeper this time. We move together until we both gasp and collapse, limbs tangled in soft sheets, breathless and buzzing.

"Wow," Ryan pants, his hand resting on my thigh.

"Wow is right," I reply, biting back a smile that can't be contained.

We lie in that quiet aftermath, his hand still grounding me, reminding me this wasn't just in my head. I glance at him, and he tilts his face toward mine.

"So... how are you feeling?" he asks softly.

"Really good," I admit. "Not just the sex. I just feel... really close to you. I want to explore this, for real."

Ryan smiles, slow and sincere. "What better place than Mexico?"

I cuddle into him, feeling like a whole new woman.

Eventually, Ryan gets up to freshen up. I follow, grabbing a soft robe from the closet. Before wrapping myself in cotton, I lather the aloe over my sunburn, the cool gel waking up my skin with goosebumps and gratitude.

Ryan peeks at me, nodding toward the bottle. "Helping at all?"

"Very much," I sigh, going in for round two of the cooling sensation.

He grabs a robe too, clearly convinced by my aloe-enhanced spa vibes. I duck into the bathroom and sit—because (say it with me, ladies), *always pee after sex*. As I go through the motions, a thought creeps in like an uninvited guest.

*Should I tell him about the figurine?*

Would he laugh? Would he think I've lost it? Would he take it back—all of this—because suddenly I'm the girl with the weird talking doll?

"You okay in there?" Ryan calls gently through the door.

"Yeah, sorry!"

I flush, wash my hands, and dry them as he adds, "I'm going to head down and book us dinner at that restaurant we missed yesterday. You good here?"

"Yes! Thank you."

The door clicks shut behind him.

Silence.

I walk over to my suitcase and unzip the pocket she's been in. My fingers find the familiar carved wood. I pull her out, the weight of her in my palm grounding and surreal.

"Do you think it's a good idea to tell him about you?" I whisper.

Nothing.

I glance toward the patio. The breeze calls to me. I step outside, letting the air play in my hair like it's dancing to the same slow rhythm my thoughts are moving to.

*Sin.*

That's what Samantha said her name was. Lust, greed, wrath, envy, sloth—she's guided me through each. But here's the thing: none of it *felt* like sin. Not really. Each moment led to clarity. To strength. To growth.

Is that really sinful?

No. It feels... *purposeful.* Like there's something I'm meant to see.

I think of Samantha—the shopkeeper, the mysterious antique sage in casual disguise. She sent me this figurine for a reason. There's a lesson I'm meant to learn. But what? That sin is actually good?

No. That can't be it... right?

"Fran?"

I gasp and spin around.

Ryan stands in the doorway, eyes narrowed. He points at the figurine still clutched to my chest.

"What's that?"

Shit.

# THIRTEEN

They say life is made up of moments. Moments that define us, shape who we are, how we react, who we love—everything. And right now, in this moment, I'm clutching the figurine with a racing heart while Ryan's curious eyes fix on my hands. This moment feels like one of those life-altering ones that decide where the road forks next.

What do I say?

Do I tell him everything?

Do I lie?

Do I stall?

"Fran?"

Too late. I've paused too long. My brain short-circuits and all I manage is: "I... I... well... it's kind of a funny story, really."

Ryan sits down on one of the two chairs overlooking the beach, nodding. "I like funny stories."

This is Ryan. *My* Ryan. He's open-minded. He'll understand... right?

"I'm just going to grab us some drinks first," I say, scrambling for time—and courage.

I bring the figurine inside with me, holding it like it might whisper a divine script into my ear. *Come on, say something. Give me a sign. Should I tell him the truth or keep you a secret?*

Nothing.

Typical.

I head to the minibar and pour two strong drinks—liquid bravery, don't fail me now. I hand one to Ryan and sit beside him, sipping deeply while taking in the sea and sand like it might steady me.

Ryan eyes me and the figurine with a raised brow. "So... that thing's got a story, huh? You didn't just grab it at the gift shop?"

I set my drink down on the tiny table and exhale. "Ryan... you might not believe me. Hell, *I* barely believe me, and I'm living it."

His expression shifts—eyebrows drawing together in a way I *do not* like. "You're kinda scaring me."

I rake my fingers through my hair. "Okay, you know I love antiques. That little shop in Dudsville? I bought this there. Ever since… strange things have happened. It talks to me. In my head. It's guided me. Helped me leave Greg, pushed me to take chances, told me to go to the casino—where I won, by the way."

I stop when I see the twitch at the corner of his mouth. He's trying not to laugh.

He glances at the figurine—still sultry, still wooden—then gives his drink a skeptical shake, as if checking for hallucinogens. "That must've been a *really* strong pour."

And just like that, my heart cracks. I should've known. Of course he doesn't believe me. I shouldn't have said anything. What was I thinking?

He leans forward, takes my hands gently. "Look, I know things have been hard lately. But I didn't realize it was affecting you like this. If you want to talk—I mean *really* talk—I have a great therapist you could—"

And that's where I tune out. *Therapist.* That's the word that breaks me.

I pull my hands away and stand, staring at the figurine like it betrayed me.

"This was a mistake," I murmur.

Ryan stiffens. "What was?"

But I don't answer. I turn, head back inside, and gently place the figurine in my suitcase. I change into a sundress, snatch the room key, and walk toward the door.

Ryan follows. "Francine—what are you doing?"

"I'm going for a walk."

He sounds exasperated now. "Why are you running?!"

I spin to face him, voice trembling. "Because I'm dealing with something no one believes is real! Not you, not anyone. But it *is* real. It's changed me. It's why I'm here with you, right now."

"You don't have to give credit to some antique, Francine," he snaps, voice sharp. "*You* did all that. *You* made those changes."

Like that's the moral of the story. Like I just needed a motivational speaker, not a magical, half-sinister wooden life coach in a corset.

I scoff. "That's not what I meant... Ugh. I'll be back."

"Francine—!"

I close the door behind me, needing space. Air. Silence. Something other than the weight of what just happened.

I keep my head down as the elevator hums toward the lobby. On the second floor, the same couple I'd seen making out in the pool joins me. Of course. They're still at it—giggling, kissing like they've discovered lips for the first time. *Seriously, have they not kissed enough today?*

I fight back tears. One escapes anyway.

As I step out, I hear the girl whisper, "Woah... is she okay?"

Am I?

I don't know.

It's not that I expected Ryan to believe me—what I said *doesn't* happen in real life. It belongs in books, movies, whispered legends about haunted heirlooms or magical antiques. Any rational person would be skeptical. But still, I wasn't expecting to feel this foolish. This...rejected.

I grab another Miami Vice—my signature heartbreak slushie now—and head down to the beach. The same one that had hosted such joy earlier today. My feet sink into the warm sand as I wander the shoreline. The waves greet me like old friends, crashing against my ankles with comforting rhythm.

I'm not mad he didn't believe me. I'm hurt that I trusted someone with a part of me, a big strange *real* part of me, and ended up feeling more alone than before.

I've been trying so hard to understand what this figurine really wants from me. What Samantha's cryptic wisdom was meant to spark. What I'm supposed to be learning. It's already hard, wandering through this mystery solo. But trying to *share* it with someone? That just made it worse.

A soccer ball hits my thigh, jolting me from my thoughts. A wide-eyed kid runs over.

"Oh my gosh, I'm so sorry!"

I smile, handing it back. "Don't worry about it. Happens to the best of us."

**Francine.**

The voice makes me gasp. I turn out to sea, pretending I'm just taking in the horizon, so no one sees me talking to what looks like absolutely nothing.

"What... did I do the right thing? Please."

***You don't give yourself enough credit. You've followed my guidance, yes. But that's all it was—guidance. Suggestions. You are the one carving your path. You made the choice to tell Ryan because it was your truth, your want. That's never wrong.***

I blink against the breeze. "So... it wasn't a mistake?"

***It was brave. And you must give him time to process.***

"Can't you... I don't know, *prove* it to him? Help him believe? Speed this up?"

***Unfortunately, no. To interfere would unravel the lesson too soon. Your path is too delicate. Too perfect to rush. You're almost there.***

"Almost there," I whisper, "almost where?"

Nothing.

Just the waves again.

But still—I feel lighter. Heard. I step into the water, letting it swirl around my calves, salty and cool and beautiful. Life is messy, even with a supernatural antique giving cryptic pep talks in your head. Even *with* that, you still get your heart bruised. Still face hard choices. Still feel alone sometimes.

But that's what makes it beautiful, isn't it?

There are infinite paths. Infinite versions of our lives, just waiting to be chosen. Being here in Mexico, with a man who truly sees me—maybe not all of me just yet, but most of me—that's one of those beautiful paths.

Let's see where it leads.

"I won't let you down," I whisper. To the figurine. To myself. To Ryan. To life.

---

I make my way back to the room, picking up two Miami Vices along the way. It feels like a peace offering. Or a redo. Or both.

The keycard clicks, unlocking the heavy door. I step inside.

Ryan's still there, standing exactly where I left him, staring out at the ocean. I wonder if he saw me on the beach… and I wonder if he hoped I'd come back.

"Ryan?"

He turns. His eyes are red.

*Was he crying?*

"Yeah?" he says softly.

I walk over and hand him one of the two cold drinks. "Here. Thought you might like another."

"You thought correct," he says, taking a huge sip like it's the antidote to the last twenty minutes.

I watch him carefully as I settle into the seat beside him on the balcony. The tension lingers, but it's softening.

"Francine," he begins, voice low, "I'm really sorry for hurting you."

His face is open, vulnerable, more than I've ever seen it.

"So am I," I admit. "Let's just…take a second and regroup."

We do. The air is filled with the ambient chaos of resort life—waves crashing, people laughing in the pool, distant squeals from someone probably trying parasailing for the first time. It's strangely grounding.

I take a long sip of my drink, then breathe deep. "Okay. I know what I said was a bit…*out there*. And I don't expect you to believe it, not completely. That's okay. I just—shared it because I trust you. A lot. You're the only person I've told."

Ryan clasps his hands, his eyes scanning mine. "I trust you too. And I know you well enough to know you're not…full of it. So when you say this thing is guiding you? That it talks to you?" He gestures loosely toward the room, toward the figurine. "You're not just making it up?"

I shake my head. "Nope. At the wedding, I wasn't sure whether to talk to you. I was still with Greg. But she—*it*—nudged me to go for it. And, well…that led us here."

Ryan raises his drink like a toast. "Then thank her for me."

I smile, not sure if he's joking or being genuine. Maybe both. "I will."

He watches me as I continue, "It's been…confusing. Weird. But I've done things I never thought I'd be brave enough to do. I've faced stuff I always avoided. This whole thing—it's helped me grow. And I'm really starting to like the woman I'm becoming."

He exhales, his whole body relaxing. "I'm glad to hear that, Francine. Really. And I'm glad we talked it out. First fight, huh?"

I smirk. "Who knew it'd be about the Woman of Sin?"

He chuckles, then adds, "I'm just glad we circled back. Communication's everything, right? Especially for people like us."

"Office nerds with feelings?" I ask, raising an eyebrow.

"Exactly." He winks.

I lean back in my chair, feeling the tension start to dissolve into something lighter. "I've been visiting the antique store too—the one where I found her. The woman who sold it to me, Samantha, she's...enigmatic. I swear she knows more than she lets on."

Ryan shrugs. "If she does, I'm sure she'll tell you when the time's right. You are moving down the street, after all."

We fall into a companionable silence, both finishing our drinks slowly. My heart is still beating fast, echoes of the emotional spike earlier, but it's better now. Steadying.

Our first real fight.

Over a seductive, magical figurine.

*That's one for the history books.*

# FOURTEEN

I wake up to the sun kissing my face—or wait, that's Ryan.

"Wakey, wakey! It's time to go home today."

I groan, rolling away from both him and the sunlight, "No. I refuse."

Ryan laughs as I hear the comforter slide off his side of the bed. "I know, the travel-day blues. It's brutal."

I flip onto my back, frowning dramatically. "Can we stay just a little longer? Please?"

"Well… if you're willing to use some of that money you won at the casino—with help from your wooden friend."

I blink at him, confused—then remember. Oh, right. He knows. About the figurine. About the... magic. Whether he actually believes me or not is still up for debate, but just saying it out loud felt incredible.

I drag myself out of bed, already dreading customs and cramped planes. As I gather up the clothes I left scattered around, my phone buzzes on the nightstand. It's a message from Betty.

*"Hey, Fran. I hope you've been feeling better. Haven't heard from you since my engagement party. I'm going dress shopping this weekend—would love it if you came! 1 p.m., here's the address."*

I wince. Yep. Bad friend behavior confirmed. I shoot her a quick reply, apologizing and promising I'll be there. Her response comes back almost instantly:

*"No worries, we all go through stuff. I'm so excited to see you!"*

Ryan wraps his arms around me from behind, his hands warm on my shoulders. "All good?"

"Yeah. Betty invited me to go wedding dress shopping with her this weekend. I've been a pretty terrible friend."

"No better time to make it right."

I nod, a little more grounded than before. Rebuilding. That's what I'll do.

I zip my suitcase with a final, reluctant tug—the kind of zip that feels like a goodbye. I slide on my Ray-Bans, taking one last look around the room.

"Well... that's that."

"That's that," Ryan echoes. "You ready?"

He means more than just the airport.

I meet his gaze. "Most definitely."

We leave behind the room where we connected, where we fought, where the truth about the Woman of Sin came out. This trip wasn't just a getaway. It was a turning point. And honestly? I wouldn't change a thing.

We hand our luggage to the shuttle driver and settle into our seats, the warm leather and faint smell of sunscreen wrapping around us. Ryan drapes an arm around me and closes his eyes.

"What are we?" I ask quietly.

His eyes open, locking onto mine. "What do you want us to be, Francine?"

"Together."

It surprises both of us—me included—but I stand by it.

He grins. "Is that so?"

I blush, but my voice stays firm. "Yeah. Let's… date. Officially. Let's see where this goes."

"Sounds good, beautiful," he says, kissing my forehead. They say men who kiss your forehead are the marrying type. Okay, slow down, Franny. Let's get through customs first.

On the plane, Ryan gives me the window seat—chivalry lives. I lean my head against the cool glass, watching the tarmac blur as we taxi.

"This was an incredible trip," I murmur. "Exactly what I needed. I feel… changed."

"I'm not ready to go back to work," Ryan groans, wrestling his carry-on into place.

"Ugh, same. I love helping people, but this trip reminded me how good it feels to help myself, too."

Ryan squeezes my hand. "And did you? Help yourself?"

I smile, interlocking my fingers with his. "Very much so."

"We're really doing this," he says. "Fran, I'm so happy. I've wanted to be with you for a long time—but I wanted to respect your space."

I lean against Ryan's shoulder, breathing in the soft, woody scent of his cologne. Instantly calming.

"And I appreciate that," I say softly. "I just figured… waiting, making excuses—none of that leads to happiness."

"Understandable," he murmurs. "Your relationship with… Greg, that's it? That wasn't easy. It was traumatic. I wouldn't have blamed you for taking more time."

"I'm good," I answer simply, pressing a small kiss to his shoulder.

**Good girl. Time to think of yourself!**

I smirk at the voice in my head—my guide, my sass-tastic light. Ryan might not fully believe in the Woman of Sin, but he didn't run either. That counts for something.

I close my eyes, letting myself imagine what life will be like once we're home: being a better friend to Betty, deepening whatever this thing is with Ryan, settling into my new place. All the changes, all the new beginnings—it's thrilling. A few months ago, this life would've felt like a fantasy. But it's not. It's real.

And I'm living it. Finally.

The jolt of the plane landing brings me back. The tires screech softly against the tarmac, and Ryan stirs beside me, blinking his eyes open.

"Ugh. How long was I out?"

"A few hours," I reply, switching off airplane mode. My phone buzzes almost instantly.

A sweet message from Betty:

*"Can't wait for this weekend!"*

I smile—surprisingly, I can't wait either.

Then another text comes in. From my mom:

*"When you're back from your trip, we need to chat."*

I read it aloud, furrowing my brows. "Huh."

"What?" Ryan echoes, stretching and unbuckling his seatbelt.

"Oh, nothing. My mom sent a weirdly cryptic message." I flash him the screen.

He raises his eyebrows. "Oh wow, yeah, that's peak mom ominous. Definitely keep me posted on that one."

"I will," I say, unclicking my own seatbelt.

We both stand—perks of sitting near the front. I glance behind us at the crowd already lining the aisle. People from row 24 rushing like they'll teleport if they hustle hard enough. Plane logic: always fascinating, rarely sensible.

We step off the aircraft, breathing in sweet, recycled-air-free oxygen. Once outside the terminal, Ryan turns to me with a smile.

"Well... I guess this is where we part ways."

I blink, suddenly bummed. Right. We took separate cars.

"Oh. Yeah. I had such a great time with you, Ryan."

"And I you," he replies, leaning in for a quick, warm kiss. "Text me after you talk to your mom. And when you're ready to see me again. I'm a hot commodity, you know."

I laugh, rolling my eyes. "Are you now?"

"Limited edition," he says with a wink, walking backward a few steps before turning to head to his car.

I watch him go, a silly grin on my face and my heart a little fuller than it was before.

I walk to my car and toss my luggage into the trunk, already dreading the return to the grind: work, home, sleep, repeat. Why couldn't we have just stayed in Mexico forever? Why haven't any of us won the lottery? Rude.

As I watch the parking machine chew up my ticket and spit out a *very* unnecessary number, I laugh internally. For someone who never buys lottery tickets, I sure spend a lot of time fantasizing about winning.

I pay with a sigh and a swipe of my credit card. With a happy little *ka-ching*, the bar lifts, and I roll forward, hitting "Call" on my mom's name. She'd been sweet before I left—unusually sweet—so I'm curious about what this cryptic follow-up is all about.

"Just kidding, you're still a failure in my eyes!" I mutter aloud in a perfect imitation of her, grinning at my own sarcasm.

"Hello, Fran. How was your trip?" she answers, her tone even and unreadable.

"Amazing, actually. I'm getting really close to my friend, Ryan. He... may be more than a friend now. He makes me happy, and I know you might disagree but—"

I pause as I hear her sigh on the other end.

"Mom?"

"Francine... did you get my text?"

"Yes, Mom. That's why I'm calling. I'm nearby—can I swing by?"

"That would be lovely," she says gently. Huh. That's not normal.

I detour toward her house, half expecting her new husband to be there. Instead, she's on the porch alone, rocking in her beloved chair, her movement smooth and slow like a metronome set to melancholy.

I get out, lock the car, and pull her into a hug. "Hey, Mom."

She smiles, and I join her on the porch, nudging the chair gently so we sway in sync.

"You've had this thing since I was born," I say with a chuckle.

"I know. I love it. I've never found another one quite as comfy," she says. "And it's sturdy. Like your mom."

I glance over at her. "So... what did you want to talk to me about?"

She sighs, eyes trained on the warm orange spill of the setting sun.

"Would you like some iced tea first?"

Oh no. **Iced tea.** The *harbinger* of bad news in our household. She handed me a glass when my hamster died. Another when Grandpa passed. No ice that time.

"You're really scaring me."

She turns, still smiling in that weird Stepford kind of way.

"I'm getting a divorce."

I blink. "Not to sound insensitive, but... that's not really new territory."

"I know, dear." Her voice dips. "The real news is... they found a lump."

A cold knot forms in my chest.

"L-lump? Where?"

"In my breast," she says, adjusting herself and giving a half-laugh. "I have an appointment next week to find out how serious it is. But I think, no matter what, I'll have to say goodbye to the girls." She pushes her boobs upward like she's joking—but her eyes don't match the tone.

Tears sting at the edges of mine. "Oh... my God. Mom, I... I'm so sorry. Are you going to be okay?"

"I think so. I hope so. Only God knows." She exhales, long and quiet. "And as for the divorce—once I realized I might be sick, I wanted to just… let go. Travel. Feel alive. But your stepfather didn't want any part of an adventurous life. So… we're done."

I lean in, wrapping my arms tightly around her. She gasps in surprise, but then holds me just as firmly. We stay like that for a moment—just two women in a quiet hug. It reminds me of those rare days when I was little and she let her guard down enough to let me in.

"How about some dinner?" she asks.

"I'm starving," I admit. All I had was a sad cookie and lukewarm coffee on the plane. Airline cuisine: never it.

She leads me inside and heads to the fridge while I settle at the kitchen table, watching her every move. There's something about this moment—something about *her*—that feels different. My mother, the one who always seemed invincible and untouchable, suddenly looks very… human. Mortal. Prone to lumps and loss and loneliness, just like the rest of us.

"Let me know if you need me to drive you to your appointment next week," I offer. "Or anything. I mean it."

She pulls out a frozen pizza and taps the preheat button on her ancient oven. "Of course, dear. I'll be fine. But… thank you." She pauses. "Now, tell me about this Ryan character."

I raise an eyebrow. *Who is this woman and what has she done with my mother?*

But I spill. I spill it *all*. About Ryan. About the trip. About how he makes me laugh and challenges me and holds me in a way no one else ever has. We giggle like we're teenagers at a sleepover, as if Ryan is some cute boy who passed me a note in study hall. She even suggests we all go out for dinner one day.

"That'd be nice," I say, genuinely touched. "Did I mention I met him at your most recent wedding?"

"Huh," she smirks, sipping her tea. "Would you look at that—finally a *positive* from one of my marriages."

For the first time in… maybe forever, I don't feel the urge to bolt after a visit with her. There's no tightness in my chest, no mental math calculating how much longer I need to stay to be polite. She sips her tea and looks at me over the rim of her mug.

"Fran… how are you really doing with Greg?"

I take a breath. "Honestly? I'm okay. I think I mourned that relationship long before I left it. He drained me. I was just… surviving. But now, with Ryan, I feel light. Free. I want to explore the world. Did you know Mexico was my first real trip in a decade?"

"I did," she nods, blowing softly on her tea. "You're more than welcome to a cup, by the way."

I shake my head. "No thanks, I should get going. Need to unpack and all that. You should come see the new house sometime."

"Oh, right," she says, squinting thoughtfully. "You moved to… Bleakville?"

I snort. "*Dusdville*, Mom. Not quite as ominous as it sounds."

"Never heard of it," she shrugs, getting up from the table.

She walks me to the door and I give her one more tight hug.

"Don't forget," I say. "If you need *anything*, I'm here. And I'll visit again soon."

"Sounds good, dear," she says with a warm smile, waving as I back out of the driveway.

# FIFTEEN

Humans are intelligent, complex creatures. We've traveled to other planets, solved some of the world's toughest philosophical questions, and—hey—we managed to invent fire.

And yet, despite decades of research and genius minds at work, we still haven't figured out cancer.

Cancer is destructive, like fire. But we figured out fire. We can contain it, use it. Cancer? Not so much. It ravages through the body like flames through a house, unrelenting, until its host dies. Which, in my opinion, is kind of stupid. Why destroy your home? Why ensure your own end? It's baffled scientists and doctors for generations.

As I park in my new driveway, I imagine some doctor's face lighting up—finally cracking the code. It happening before my mom gets her results, though? Highly unlikely.

I drag my suitcase inside, up the stairs, and throw it on the bed. It stares at me like it dares me to unpack it. But laundry doesn't do itself. Ugh.

I round up the dirty clothes and dump them into the machine. It chirps its little "I'm starting now" song like it's about to drop the beat at a club instead of spinning my socks. I roll my eyes and walk to the closet, where a few unpacked boxes still sit on the floor like squatters.

I groan. Boxes and laundry—the evil twins of adulthood. With nothing else on the agenda before Betty's bridal appointment tomorrow, I resign myself to productivity. Post-vacation life hits hard. One day you're sipping margaritas on a beach, the next you're elbow-deep in fabric softener.

As I slice open the boxes, I start thinking about the casino winnings. Should I invest? Toss it into stocks? A TFSA? Maybe I should just start stuffing it in mason jars like an old-timey prospector. I pull out a cute floral dress—perfect for tomorrow—and lay it on the bed.

By the time I finish unpacking, the sun's dipped below the horizon. Crickets chirp, the sound of Dudsville settling in for the night. The name's misleading—the last thing this town feels like is a dud.

It feels like…home.

Homesville.

I sip wine on the back porch, listening to the occasional car pass, watching moths perform aerial ballet around the porch light. Peaceful, grounded, still. For now.

I step into the bridal shop—**Brides and Babes**—a glittering wonderland of white. Satin and lace and tulle gowns sparkle from every corner, some sleek and slinky, others puffed up like marshmallows on steroids. One of them actually winks at me. Or maybe I'm sleep-deprived. Who's to say?

Then I hear it—Betty's signature laugh, loud and unfiltered. I follow the sound around a corner and there she is, striking a pose and clearly mocking someone or something. Two women sit on a plush U-shaped couch, giggling at her antics.

"Betty," I call out, grinning.

The trio turns. I don't recognize the other two, but Betty squeals, "Fran, you're here!"

She rushes over and hugs me tight. I laugh, hugging her back. "Of course I am. I wouldn't miss this."

They stand as Betty gestures to a tall blonde with legs for days. "This is Piper. I've known her since university, but she travels a lot—like, 'might be in Bali tomorrow' a lot—so it's extra special she's here today."

Piper and I exchange polite smiles and nods. Then Betty turns to the other woman: a shy brunette with oversized glasses, practically the anti-Piper in every way.

"And this is Miranda—my cousin and the closest family member I have. And guys, this is Francine. We met at my first-ever job slinging overpriced lattes."

"Amazing to meet you," Miranda says softly, her voice barely rising over the boutique's soundtrack of ambient harp music. "We're so excited for Betty."

"Yeah," Piper agrees, flopping gracefully back into her seat. "She deserves this moment. Now... where's our dress whisperer?"

I sit down with them as Betty starts browsing the walls of wedding gowns like a kid in a candy store, "oohing" and "aahing" at literally every single one.

"Betty," I call out with a smirk, "do you even have a *type* of dress in mind?"

She turns, holding up two gowns in each hand like she's in some sparkly duel. "I mean... I love the idea of a poofy ball gown. Feels very 'once upon a time.' But those sleek ones with the trains? They're so regal. I'm torn!"

Piper giggles. "This is why we're here. You try on everything. One will just click—you'll *know*."

"That's what they all say," Betty sighs dramatically, just as a boutique employee strides up in heels that scream authority.

"Hi, ladies! Who's the bride?"

Betty raises her hand like she's answering a pop quiz, and the woman grins. "Perfect. Welcome! I'm Sasha, and I'll be helping you find *the* dress. And who are the babes?" She gestures to us.

We all raise our hands like a sparkly bridal army.

"Excellent," Sasha nods. "Alright, bride-to-be, talk to me. Any dress ideas so far?"

Betty shrugs, clearly overwhelmed. "I think I need to try everything. I love the drama of a ball gown, but those fitted ones are stunning too..."

Sasha chuckles. "Totally normal. Happens to the best of us. Alright—do you like lace? Sparkle? Sleeves? Illusions?"

As Betty starts narrowing down the details, I glance around the shop. Other brides are crying into tissue boxes with their moms, having their *say yes to the dress* moment. Others look like they're about to throw a tulle tantrum. It's a whole spectrum of bridal energy.

And I can't help but wonder... will I ever be here someday? With my mom? Or... not?

Sasha eventually leads Betty into a changing room, the two disappearing with a wave and a handful of hangers.

"I think she'll rock a full ball gown," Piper says, pulling a massive purse onto her lap and digging out a pack of gum.

"I vote mermaid," Miranda adds, twirling a strand of her hair. "She's got the curves for it—she should show them off."

They both turn to me, clearly expecting me to pick a side.

But I don't do sides.

I shrug. "Honestly? She'll look incredible in anything. Let's see how she *feels* in them."

They nod, slightly impressed, slightly disappointed I didn't take the bait. Meanwhile, I sit back, ready for the inevitable bridal whirlwind. This is Betty, after all. If she doesn't emerge from that dressing room dramatically, is she even Betty?

Sasha emerges from the dressing room, clapping like a game show host who's just awarded a cruise.

"She looks *amazing!* Come on out, sweetie!"

Betty steps out in a massive ball gown, shimmering under the boutique lights. The skirt glitters with every move, the bodice cinched like a corset straight out of a fairy tale.

"W-wow, Betty," I say first, stunned. "You look incredible."

She steps onto the pedestal, twirling slightly as the three-way mirror reflects her from every angle. Her face goes soft, thoughtful. "I *knew* it. This is going to be the hardest decision of my life."

"This one feels like it was made for you," Piper says, tucking her gum in its wrapper and dropping it delicately into her bag.

*Ew,* I think. But okay.

"Yeah, I agree," Miranda nods. "But I still want to see you in a mermaid gown."

"Oh, she's not done yet," Sasha laughs, already ushering Betty back into the changing room. "We can circle back to this one later if it's still the top contender."

As they vanish behind the curtain, I find myself mentally cataloguing my own bridal style. Simple, boho, soft lace maybe. Not all this glitter. I imagine Ryan at the end of an aisle, dressed in a perfectly tailored black—or maybe dark gray—tux, hands clasped, eyes only on me. I picture Betty there too, giving me a playful nudge, whispering, *look at him.*

I blink myself back to reality just as Betty returns, now wrapped in a show-stopping mermaid gown. The fitted bodice hugs her curves like it was sewn onto her body, while the skirt explodes into layers of tulle.

"Oh my God, Betty," Piper whistles. "You have the kind of body that looks good in *anything.* Seriously—fuck you."

This, coming from a woman built like a runway model. Right.

Betty laughs, climbing onto the pedestal again. "Oh, hush. But I mean… yeah. If you got it, flaunt it, right?"

We all nod, watching as she studies herself.

"I think I wanna try that first one on again," she says, pointing over her shoulder. "Then I'll decide for sure."

A few minutes later, she re-emerges—not in the ball gown, but in a third dress. A boho-style gown with a lace top and soft pleated skirt. Understated. Elegant. My kind of dress, honestly.

Betty twirls slowly in front of the mirror, contemplative.

I love it. I already know the others don't.

Piper pipes up—pun unintended but hilarious in my own head—"I think we should revisit the first one."

"I was thinking the same thing!" Betty grins, giving a dramatic twirl before skipping back into the dressing room, the boho dress fluttering behind her.

Piper makes a face once she's gone. "Yeah... that definitely wasn't it."

"I thought it was cute," Miranda says with a small shrug. "Simple. Sweet."

Thanks, Miranda. You've got taste.

When Betty returns—ball gown back in full glory—Miranda actually gasps.

"There she is! I seriously think this is *the* one. Can you believe the first one ended up being it?"

"I know," Betty beams, practically glowing. "But I'm here for it. This is it."

"Yay!" Sasha claps, clearly invested in her commission—and the love story, maybe. She hands Betty a veil, and when Betty puts it on, Miranda sniffles.

"My gosh... you look absolutely stunning, hun."

"You really do," I say, smiling. "Exquisite princess."

Betty takes one last look at herself in the mirror, then sighs happily. "Thanks, girls. I'm getting the veil too. Go big or go home, right?"

Betty emerges from the changing room, dressed back in her regular clothes as we all stretch like we just survived a marathon. Honestly, I'm glad the appointment wrapped up quicker than I expected. I always thought bridal appointments dragged on for hours—I was halfway to mentally drafting a group snack run.

She heads to the counter, paying the deposit, and we all file out into the warm afternoon air. Piper and Miranda walk ahead, chattering, while I sidle up beside Betty.

"Hey… where's your mom?" I keep my voice soft. I'd noticed her absence, but didn't want to bring it up mid-sparkly-dress-montage. Betty's mom can be a touchy subject. Like mine.

"Oh," she says with a shrug, "she's on a trip with her new beau. She said she'll be there for the final fitting and pay the rest then."

"Oh, that's good then!" I smile, genuinely happy for her. It's…refreshing when moms actually show up—even if it's a little delayed.

Suddenly Piper gasps, pointing at a nearby building. "No *way!* I used to sneak in here all the time when I was underage. They always let me in."

Miranda squints at the place, one brow raised. "Is it even *open?*"

I walk up to the door, peering in. "Yeah, there's people inside. Anyone hungry?"

Everyone agrees in unison. We head in and immediately get hit with the musty charm of a once-country bar turned diner. The vinyl booths squeak. The lighting is *almost* too yellow. It's perfect.

We slide into a booth, and Miranda makes a face, holding up a laminated menu like it's a biohazard. "Oh, God. Look at this."

Piper leans in, reading aloud: "'If you and your friends can finish this meal in under an hour, you walk out without paying! Are *you* up to the challenge?'" She claps her hands together. "Ohhh, girls, can we?!"

We all stare at her.

"Uh," Miranda says, her tone as dry as toast, "no offense, but you don't exactly scream *eating competition*. Your whole vibe is more…low-fat smoothies and overpriced matcha."

Piper lets out a full-belly laugh. "Fair! But I used to do these challenges with my brother when I was younger. Back when he was still around."

"I'm so sorry," I say automatically.

She waves it off. "Oh, no. He's just moved away. The jerk."

Well. Whoops.

"I mean…" Betty shrugs, "I'm *down* if everyone else is. But I should probably be on a diet if I want to fit into that dress again."

"Exactly," I say, lifting my water. "I've got a bridesmaid dress to squeeze into."

"Oh, *please,* you're a stick," Piper rolls her eyes. "You make *me* look like Jabba the Hutt."

I roll my eyes as the table erupts in laughter. Why are skinny girls always like this?

We agree—somehow—and flag down the waitress. We order water all around. Lots and lots of water. I'm going to need it.

**Come on, Fran.**

I choke on my drink, sputtering slightly as that now-familiar inner figurine voice echoes in my head.

"You okay, Francine?" Betty asks, raising an eyebrow.

I nod at Miranda. "Y-yeah. Water just went down the wrong way."

*I know you don't do this kind of thing,* the voice murmurs again. ***But it's a bonding moment. A little bit of gluttony never hurt anyone, right?***

Gluttony. Another sin.

As the waitress places a *huge* pizza down in front of us, greasy and glorious, something clicks in my mind. The seven sins. I try to remember them all—and realize, with a weird jolt—I've committed every single one.

Now what?

"Come on, Fran! Time is ticking!" Betty urges, already mid-bite.

I grab my first slice. It's still too hot but I don't care. I take a bite, the cheese stretching like it's auditioning for a commercial. I chew slowly, thinking: Even though I've committed sin, I've never been happier. That can't possibly be the lesson the antique is trying to teach me... right?

I'm not religious. Not even close. But even I know that unchecked jealousy and rage, giving in to every impulse—these are *bad* things. Aren't they?

Still, I reach for my second slice.

Maybe Samantha has more answers. Maybe it's time I stop waiting and actually *ask* for them.

"Holy shit, bride-to-be," Piper laughs. "You're already on your fourth!"

Betty just shrugs, chewing happily. "Saving money is always a good idea. *Also*: pizza."

We finish the monster pie with minutes to spare. The waitress returns and stops the timer with a grin. "Congrats, guys!"

We still leave a tip, because... we're not *monsters*. Just full.

Outside, I clutch my stomach like it might actually burst. "That was way too much cheese in one sitting."

"There is *never* too much cheese," Miranda replies, deadly serious, despite clearly being in the same mozzarella-induced distress.

We part ways at our cars, still laughing. Betty hooks her arm around mine.

"Thanks, Fran."

"For?"

"For coming out today. Doing that ridiculous contest. Honestly... it meant a lot to me."

I hug her tightly. "Of course. And like I said before—I'm sorry for how I've been. We really do need to catch up. You have to come see my new place."

Her face lights up. "Oh, that sounds awesome! Maybe Phil can come too?"

I originally wanted it to be a girls' night, but I shrug. "Whatever works."

We say our goodbyes, and I drive home, stomach still groaning from the carb overload.

"Sorry," I whisper to it, as if it can hear me.

*Must've hurt. Still, I'm proud of you. Look how far you've come.*

I park in my driveway and sigh, resting my head back for a second.

"Hey, you," I say out loud, to no one in particular. "I have a few questions."

Silence.

Of course.

I go into my house, up the stairs, and find her exactly where I left her—perched on my bedside table like a smug little gargoyle. Not a millimeter out of place.

"Hey, woman of Sin. Listen."

*Yes?*

I blink. "Huh. That worked faster than usual."

I sit on the edge of the bed, eyeing her carefully. "So… it seems I've done all the sins. Gluttony was the last, and I won't lie, it came with cheese and regret. But…I feel good. Like, genuinely satisfied with my life. What now?"

Silence.

I start to wonder if I broke some kind of ancient rule by asking. Maybe she doesn't answer existential questions. Maybe I need to stick to sins and snacking.

Then, her voice returns.

*You have almost come to your conclusion in your journey, dear Francine. I can say with complete honesty... you've been one of my most enjoyable clients. We must depart soon. Not quite yet, though.*

Depart?

"...Do I just bring you back to Samantha at the antique store?"

*Yes. Secrets will be revealed, and all will become clear.*

I pause, heart thudding.

"S-secrets?"

And then—nothing. Like a light switch flipped off.

# SIXTEEN

My phone rings just as I finish up dinner, waiting for Betty, Phil, and Ryan to arrive. My first double date since high school—and my heart is racing like I'm about to get graded on it. I turn down the stove to a simmer and answer, "Hi, Mom?"

"Hi, Francine. I just got back from my appointment."

I set the spatula down and gasp. "Oh my… right. Are you okay? What did they say? Are you—"

"If you'd let me speak, I'll tell you," she chuckles gently. I stop immediately. "Sorry. Go ahead."

She takes a deep breath.

That's never a good sign.

"Well, they said it was cancerous," she says, and my vision blurs before she adds, "but they caught it in time. I'm going in next week to have it—and my breasts—removed."

"I…" I trail off, searching for words through the sudden fog of worry. "Okay. I'm really glad they caught it early. And thank you for calling me. I'll drive you to the hospital—and take you home, too."

"Thank you, dear. Anyway, I've got to go sign the separation agreement today, so I'll talk to you later."

"I love you," I say quickly before she can hang up.

"I love you too, Francine."

We disconnect, and right then, the doorbell rings. I shut off the stove and make my way to the door, trying to shove the flood of emotion down into something manageable. Ryan stands on the porch step, holding a bouquet of flowers. For a second, I'm taken back to the bridal salon—dreaming of him at the end of an aisle.

"Thanks, Ryan," I smile. "Come in."

I lead him into the kitchen as he takes in the space. "Damn, this house looks like a real home now. And it smells incredible. I had no idea you could cook."

"Me neither," I laugh. "I always thought frozen lasagna was the height of culinary convenience. Turns out, home-cooked meals are actually fun. And… I dunno. Kind of fulfilling."

Ryan steps closer and pulls me into a hug, making me squeal in surprise. "I know this is still new," he says, "but I'd like a kiss."

I blush. "Right."

I kiss him, soft and slow, his hands moving up my arms to cradle my face. My cheeks burn under his touch, but I'm smiling before we even pull apart.

"Do you think we have time before they get here?" he asks, smirking.

I go to answer, but the doorbell chimes again—a classic cock block. "Nope."

Ryan groans exaggeratedly as I head to the door. Betty and Phil are grinning, a huge bottle of red wine in Betty's hands.

"Oh yes!" she cheers.

"See? Red was the better choice. Look at that excitement," Betty says smugly to Phil, who rolls his eyes toward the heavens. They come in and slip off their shoes.

"Wow, it smells great in here," Phil says, nodding at the stove. "Excited to eat something other than my fiancée's cooking."

Betty gasps. "You *love* my cooking."

"I love *you*," he says, pecking her lips.

Usually I'd want to puke, but honestly? I smile.

"Oh! Right," I say, gesturing to Ryan. "Everyone—this is Ryan. Ryan, this is Betty and Phil. They're getting married soon."

"Exciting," Ryan says, reaching out for a handshake. "Nice to meet you both. Want a beer, Phil?"

"That would be amazing," Phil replies as they head into the kitchen like old friends already.

I laugh quietly to myself. Ryan offering drinks from *my* fridge like he lives here already. Weirdly, I don't mind.

Betty sidles up beside me, eyes wide with a grin. "Wow. He's so cute."

"Slow down," I tease. "You're the one getting married."

She clicks her tongue and smacks my arm playfully. I plate the pasta onto the nice dishes I haven't touched since college. We all sit down at the table, and for the first time in a long time, I feel like I'm exactly where I'm meant to be.

"Parmesan, please!" Ryan says.

I hand him the cheese and dig in. It's actually *good*. Like, surprisingly good. I found this recipe in an old cookbook my mom gave me years ago—the one with the tattered corners and coffee stains. It had a dog-eared page with this pasta dish, and I figured… why not?

"So, do you guys like it?" I ask, trying to play it cool but failing spectacularly.

"Amazing," Phil says, nodding with genuine surprise. "Pasta usually bores me, but this—the spices, the texture—everything is perfect. We may have to steal the recipe."

Betty enthusiastically agrees. "Yeah, love, this is seriously delicious. You've clearly been holding out on us!"

I laugh, brushing a strand of hair behind my ear as Ryan places his hand on top of mine. "Delicious, my love."

Betty smiles at the two of us as we finish our plates. Once everyone's wiped their mouths and leaned back in satisfied silence, I pull out the pièce de résistance: apple pie with vanilla bean ice cream—my absolute favorite.

"You are *spoiling* us," Betty squeaks, happily scooping a generous dollop of ice cream onto her plate.

"Only the best for the best," I grin, serving up the rest. They dig in like they haven't eaten in days, and halfway through, Phil looks up at me thoughtfully.

"Fran… it really seems like you're doing so much better since Greg. We didn't realize how much he was holding you back. We're so sorry."

I shake my head as I reach for the wine they brought. "No, no. None of that is on you. I was the one clinging to the idea it would somehow get better."

Phil turns to Ryan. "You're okay with us bringing this up?"

"Of course," Ryan says with a nod. "It's all part of her story—and I care about all of it."

"What a catch," Betty murmurs, smiling at Ryan.

Phil side-eyes her, and we all burst out laughing.

Betty shakes her head, serious again. "Relationships with substance abuse are... well, they're hard. A vicious cycle. We're so proud of you, Fran. I can't even imagine what you went through."

I lift the wine bottle and gesture with it. "Okay, first off, none of that 'I should have done more' stuff. You didn't rub your relationship in my face. You were happy, and that's nothing to apologize for. I'm proud of *you*, too."

Betty's eyes soften. Ryan leans back in his chair and adds, "It's wild, really—how much a single person can change us. We see that in our work all the time, but when you live it... it still feels unbelievable."

Phil nods. "And then the glow after you've escaped? It's instant. You're literally glowing in this cute little house, Franny."

I smirk, sipping my wine. "Don't let that get to your head. But thanks."

We move the party to the backyard. Betty takes one look at the twinkling fairy lights I strung up and gasps. "Girl, this is *adorable*. Phil, pack your things—we're moving in."

We all laugh, settling into the patio chairs as the sun dips lower.

"So," Phil says, "tell us about this Mexico trip!"

Ryan perks up, pulling out his phone to show off pictures. There's one of us on the beach, waves crashing in the background, and another of us dancing at a club—sweaty, smiling, with my hair sticking to my forehead and pure joy stretched across my face.

"This one's my favorite of Francine," Ryan says, showing them the photo.

Betty clasps her hands together. "You look so happy. So free."

I smile at the image. "I really do, don't I?"

Ryan takes a sip of wine, his eyes sparkling with mischief. "The craziest thing happened while we were there…"

I raise a brow, instantly suspicious. There wasn't anything *that* crazy that—wait.

Oh no. He wouldn't.

I look at his slightly buzzed expression.

Oh yes. He *would*.

"What happened?" Betty leans forward like it's the dramatic peak of a soap opera.

"Francine told me a magical artifact has been guiding her for the past few months," Ryan says, turning toward me with a smile that freezes as he catches the horror on my face. "Ultimately helping her become who she is now."

Silence.

Then Phil chuckles. "I don't even know what to say to that. What kind of tequila are they serving down there, and where do I sign up?"

I glare at Ryan, heat rising to my cheeks, and stand up. "I'll… be back."

"Wait, Fran—" Ryan calls after me, but I'm already heading inside.

I pour myself a fresh glass of wine and head upstairs, letting the door click shut behind me. I sit on my bed, seething and embarrassed. My eyes land on the Woman of Sin figurine, still perched smugly on my nightstand like she hasn't moved in centuries.

Still as seductive and infuriating as ever.

"Why can't I have *your* body?" I mutter at her, sipping the wine.

There's a knock at my door. Soft. Hesitant.

"Fran?"

I groan, taking a big gulp of wine. The bitter sting hits my throat but somehow feels good. Ryan appears in the doorway, leaning casually against the frame, a worried crease forming between his brows. We hold each other's gaze until he bites his lip.

"Can I… come in?"

I shrug. "You apparently call the shots, so go ahead."

He winces but stays put. "I'm sorry. I had way too much to drink. I don't know why I said what I did—or even brought it up. It wasn't my place."

I cross my legs, setting my glass of wine carefully in the center of the bed. Turning to look at him seriously, I say, "It's not just what you said. It's how you made me look… like I'm stupid. Insane. Crazy."

Ryan steps fully into the room, moving closer to the bed. "I know. And trust me, I'm so sorry."

His eyes catch the Woman of Sin figurine perched on my bedside table. He reaches out to touch it. "Wow. The detail is amazing up close."

I hide a smirk as he keeps studying it. "You said… she talks to you? Guides you?"

I nod. "Yes, Ryan. We don't need to get into it. I get why you don't believe me. Honestly, who would?"

"Why does she only talk to you?"

"Because she's helping me," I reply, as if I actually know why. The truth is, I have no idea why she doesn't guide the people around me.

"I could use some magical wood helping me out," Ryan jokes, gently placing the figurine back down. He frowns, watching me finish my wine. "Fran, I really am sorry. That was totally uncalled for. Please, come back downstairs."

I stand, stretching. "Okay. But only because I want more wine."

Ryan smirks, seeing right through me, and follows me downstairs. I pour more wine and step back outside. "Hey guys. Sorry about that."

Phil waves it off. "Not to worry. We were just discussing our honeymoon plans."

"Oh yeah? Where'd you decide?"

"Turks and Caicos," Betty beams. "White sandy beaches, tropical drinks. What more could you want?"

"Old architecture, history, European food," Phil counters, making Betty stare at him like he's crazy.

"Well… I guess we haven't decided yet," he admits with a laugh.

Phil wraps an arm around Betty, who rolls her eyes but snuggles closer.

"You two are so cute, I might actually barf," I joke, winking at them.

Betty glances inside. "So are you and Ryan. Where is he?"

"I'm not sure…" I trail off just as the door opens and Ryan steps out, brushing his hands on his pants.

"Where did you go?"

Ryan sits beside me. "Figured I'd do the dishes real quick. Saves the hassle later."

"Oh girl, marry him! Phil doesn't even do that."

We both blush, looking down at our shoes.

# SEVENTEEN

I step into the office, my boots clicking sharply on the floor. The familiar scent of cheap coffee and the low hum of workday dread settle around me like a cozy, annoying blanket. I drop my purse on the desk just as Barry rounds the corner, spotting me instantly. He smiles, waving, then slips the door closed behind him.

"Barry. How was it without me?" I tease.

"Honestly? The building almost burned down once," he says deadpan.

I roll my eyes. "Oh, dear."

He winks. "You think I'm kidding."

"How was your trip?" Barry asks, eyes on me as I prepare for my upcoming air time.

"Really great, actually. Didn't realize how much I missed doing absolutely nothing in the sun until I was there. Why did I wait so long to take a vacation?"

Barry hops up onto my desk. "It's easy to get caught in the grind. I'm glad you got some rest—you deserve it. Ready for your show?"

I nod, smoothing out my notes. "Yeah. I've got a new development in my love life, so I'm sharing some thoughts on that."

Barry raises an eyebrow. "O-oh? You and Greg…" he trails off, eyes curious.

I settle into my chair, smirking. "Definitely not Greg. He's way out of the picture. Ryan—the guy from that special you brought in? Well, we knew each other before, and things…clicked."

"Interesting," Barry nods slowly. "Anyway, enjoy your first day back!"

I sign in, hear Barry's voice introduce me as usual, and take a deep breath.

"Welcome back, everyone! I'm sure you've all missed me as much as I've missed you. A girl needs her vacation, though, right? I've got some juicy updates: your girl Francine is finally letting a new man in. After a rocky breakup with my ex-fiancé, I'm opening the door to someone else. A word of advice: don't expect every new person to be like your ex—they just aren't. Trauma and heartbreak are real, but don't let them rob you of amazing opportunities with amazing people. Now, let's see who our first caller is!"

My heart races, as always, when I get personal. I key in the first call.

"Hello! You're live. Go ahead!"

"Hi, Francine! You're such an inspiration!"

"Aw, thank you—that's so kind!"

"My problem is pretty standard: I love my hobbies, my husband loves his. But we don't share any interests. Is that… concerning?"

I ask, "First, what's your name? I like to make things personal."

"Layla."

"Gorgeous name. Layla, having different hobbies can actually be healthy—it helps keep individuality. But no shared interests at all? That can be a red flag. A healthy relationship needs some common ground—like reading a book together, or monthly poker nights. Have you talked about what you might enjoy doing together?"

There's silence on the line, and I start to wonder if she dropped off, but then she replies,

"We tried, but that day we were both too frustrated. Every idea one of us suggested, the other shot down. We were exhausted from not…connecting."

I respond, "Here's what I suggest: try that conversation again, but really listen this time. Write down all your ideas separately, with reasons why you like them. Then share your lists. It might help you both see possibilities and feel more connected instead of distant."

"That sounds good, Fran. It'd break my heart if we split up."

"I believe you. Use that—channel it into working through this and finding some middle ground with him. I truly believe you'll discover something that strengthens your bond."

Layla signs off, and I lean back, a small, satisfied smile playing on my lips. Another little win. Another love story with a shot at a happy ending.

I've known since I was a kid that I loved helping people navigate relationships. My first unofficial "client" was Preena—my beautiful, wildly dramatic best friend in middle school. She was head-over-heels for this boy in our grade, and at just thirteen, I was already giving her pep talks and writing half her texts. And it worked—they lasted longer than most adult relationships I know.

And then there's my mom. Watching her cycle through one marriage after another like they were seasonal hobbies? Yeah, that planted a seed too. I didn't want to just help people *find* love. I wanted to help them *keep* it. Fulfillment. Happiness. Something that sticks.

It all circles back to when I first pitched this radio show to Barry.

---

"Barry, please, just hear me out," I said, hot on his heels like an eager intern chasing a dream—and maybe a promotion.

He sighed. "Fran, you know we've been scrambling around here, trying to come up with ways to boost listeners."

I closed the office door behind him, leaning on it like a woman on a mission. "Exactly. And if you just listen for five minutes, you'll see this has *everything* to do with that."

He dropped into his chair, running a hand through his hair. The man looked two coffees and a breakdown deep. "Fine," he groaned. "Go."

I pushed off the door, arms crossed like a CEO-in-training. "I know I've only been here six months and that I'm 'just the coffee girl' or whatever—"

"You said it, not me."

"—but I have a killer idea," I said, holding up a finger. "Relationships."

He blinked. "Sorry, what?"

"Relationships! The one thing every single person listening can relate to. Marriage, siblings, parents, exes, awkward work crushes. And what's the common thread? They're all complicated. What if we start a segment—no, a whole *show*—where listeners call in, ask for advice, and I help them out? Real talk. Real people. Instant engagement."

Barry peered at me over his laptop, lacing his fingers together. "Hmm. I mean... there's potential. But you've mostly been handling admin and studio coffees. Why wouldn't I give this to Georgina?"

Internally, I shriveled up and died. Outwardly, I smiled through gritted teeth and refrained from smacking him with a stapler.

"Because I *get* this," I said. "I studied it. I've lived it. I know how to talk to people. Please, Barry... just take a chance. I won't let you down."

He sighed the sigh of a man already regretting his better judgment. "I'll think about it. Be ready if we move forward."

I lit up like a Christmas tree. "You got it. Thank you!"

---

Now, sitting here, I can't help but smile at the memory. I almost didn't say anything—thought I was too new, too young, too green. But Barry? He must've seen something in me, because two days later he came back with, "You've got meetings with marketing. We're building the face of your show."

It all worked out. Not because it just *does*, but because I *asked*. I *tried*. And that's the lesson.

If you don't go for it—if you let doubt steer the ship—your life won't shape up to be what you want. And honestly, isn't *that* the real heartbreak?

**Absolutely.**

I nod subtly as the figurine agrees with my internal monologue. It's become second nature now—her silent nods, the way her presence seems to hum when I'm on the right track. I answer a few more calls, feeling genuinely content. My job, my relationships, even my sanity feel oddly intact for once. But one thing keeps gnawing at me:

What's the deal with this figurine?

What are its secrets? Why me? And why hasn't she said a single thing about going back to the store? I'm impatiently waiting for her to announce it's time, like she's some enchanted Uber driver with one cryptic destination. But...nothing. Not a peep.

As the workday wraps up, I lock my office door and turn to Barry. "Wow. That flew by."

"It really did," he says, sliding in beside me as we head for the exit. He locks up with his master key and turns to me, sighing with the weight of someone who's survived another Monday. "Great first day back, Fran. We really missed you."

Walking toward our cars, I hear faint sirens in the distance, slicing through the late-day calm. "Thanks," I say, stretching my shoulders. "I missed helping people."

"I bet you missed the sun more," he quips.

I laugh. "You're not wrong."

Barry gives me a warm look, one that softens even more as he says, "Hey...you look good, Fran. I'm happy for you. This new guy, this new place... it suits you."

"Yeah...I feel good," I admit. "Thanks, Barry."

We part ways, and my car winds its familiar route back to my cozy little haven in Dudsville—a town that somehow feels more like home than anywhere ever has. Its quiet charm and eerie stillness wrap around me like a warm quilt made by a grandma with secrets.

Halfway home, I decide to stop for groceries. Betty and Phil's whirlwind visit left my fridge looking like a sad bachelor's. I pull into the lot, grab a cart that, of course, has a wheel that drags like a ghost with unfinished business, and head inside.

The store is bright and buzzing with the usual suspects: frazzled parents, indecisive college kids, and locals who treat this store like a weekly social mixer. I head straight to produce. Celery, carrots, broccoli—check. All those hopeful, healthful foods that, let's be honest, will be rotting behind the cheese drawer by Thursday. But hey, I'm trying.

"Francine?"

I turn mid-cucumber check and see Samantha—the antique shop owner—standing across the aisle. Her small frame is almost swallowed by a floral shawl and those iconic owl-like glasses.

"Samantha!" I beam. "Nice to see you."

She smiles, her eyes twinkling with something I can't quite place. "What brings you to this humble little grocery chain in Dudsville?"

I place the cucumber back down—commitment issues, clearly. "I actually moved here a few weeks ago."

Her expression brightens, as if I just confirmed a hunch she's had since the dawn of time. "Ah, I knew it would get you. Dudsville has teeth."

"Yeah, it definitely sunk them in," I say with a laugh.

Samantha leans in slightly, studying me. "Let me guess... the little house down the road? With the longer driveway and the red shutters?"

I blink. "Uh... yeah, actually. That's the one."

She nods slowly, knowingly. "Of course it is."

Of course it is? Excuse me, cryptic queen, come again?

I nod, brushing off how strangely specific her guess had been. "You are correct. Great guess."

Samantha winks and glances down at her cart—an odd but relatable mix of healthy items tossed among chips, cookies, and what looked suspiciously like off-brand cereal marshmallows. "Well... I guess I better get back to the mundane joys of grocery shopping. Gotta love the day-to-day, right?"

"Oh, for sure," I smirk, wheeling my own wonky cart forward. "We've got to eat."

"We do," she agrees, lifting her palms with a flair of theatrical frustration, "but wouldn't it be *divine* if food just appeared? As if by magic, right on my doorstep."

I pat my phone in my back pocket. "Actually, there's an app for that."

Samantha chuckles, her expression somewhere between amused and terrified. "Me and technology? Not the best match."

Considering her shop didn't even have a cash register, just a dusty old ledger and a bell that sounded like it belonged in a haunted hotel, I believe her.

"It *is* handy," I say. "Especially when you really don't want to leave the house. Anyway, I should get back—nice seeing you!"

I start to turn, but her hand lifts in a slow, deliberate wave. "Wait… how's it going with my wooden woman?"

I pause mid-step, instantly flushing. "Great, actually. I've, uh… apparently been guided through all the sins now. I was wondering what else I needed to learn."

Samantha shrugs casually, like she isn't talking about a possibly haunted doll that reads souls for breakfast. "If she isn't done with you, then she isn't."

I tilt my head, narrowing my eyes. "Okay but—she said secrets would be revealed when I brought her back to *you*. Now that I think of it… why would I need to bring her back at all? I bought her. I own her."

Samantha only smiles, that serene, creepy, not-at-all-comforting smile of hers. "That will be answered in time."

"Oh come *on*," I groan. "She's allowed to be secretive. You? You *could* help me out, you know."

Her gaze darts side to side like we're in a spy film and the teenager texting near the bananas might be an undercover agent. She leans in slightly, voice low. "You think a certain way. You doubt if it's sin. You will be shown the truth very, very soon. You've been so patient, Francine. Trust me when I say this: *you are not doing wrong.*"

Cryptic as fuck. As always.

"Wow, Samantha. *So* helpful," I say, full sarcasm with just enough smile to stay civil.

She laughs—full, throaty, unapologetic. "You kill me, Francine. We'll meet again very soon, with her guidance. But until then, drop by the store anytime."

"I was actually thinking of picking up some more antiques for the new place," I say. "So yeah—you'll see me again."

She nods like she already knew that, of course she did, and then disappears into the baking aisle like a prophet in search of flour.

I groan, turning back to my cart, suddenly craving all the junk food in the building. I just want *answers.* I want to know the point of all this—why the figurine, why the riddles, why me. I know she's helped guide me onto a better path, one filled with real love and actual happiness, but come on. Haven't I done that already? Haven't I *graduated?*

I feel steady. Sure. Like I'm finally on the path I was meant to walk. So why do I feel like the figurine is *messing* with me now? Like she knows it's time to go back to the store but is choosing to play the long game just for fun.

***Your journey needs to continue in helping others like yourself—other lost souls.***

Oh, makes total sense, magical wooden object. I push the cart down the aisle, eyes glazed over, thinking way too hard in a grocery store. Why does she help others with nothing in return? Shouldn't there be a catch? A trade? A cursed monkey paw situation?

Oh God... did I accidentally agree to some weird demon deal? Like, "Step right up and sell your soul for emotionally stable personal growth!"

***Calm down, love. I'm not a demon. Nor do we have any kind of deal. I pride myself on honesty.***

I snort out loud. A nearby mom glances at me with that classic *stranger-danger-but-make-it-socially-polite* look. Realizing I'm not wearing headphones and appear to be chatting with my produce, she ushers her son away like I'm about to start reciting prophecies.

Sure, honesty. If you're so honest, why do I still have no idea what the end goal is? Or what these so-called "secrets" are?

***If things are spoken prematurely, lessons won't be learned. Takeaways won't be had. And happiness won't be earned. We are almost there.***

I tilt my head up at the ceiling, letting out the exhale of a woman at the end of her rope and nowhere near the end of her to-do list. I toss some ice cream into the cart. Don't judge me—my life is literally magical chaos. I've earned this tub of emotional support mint chip.

In line, I spot Samantha checking out. She winks. I wave. I try not to look like I'm internally screaming. I start unloading my items, marveling at how "just a few things" has somehow translated to $50 more than I expected. Note to self: do *not* grocery shop hungry unless you're also budgeting for impulse decisions and existential dread.

I pack the car with far too many bags, make the responsible choice to return my cart (even though the wind *almost* convinced me to let it ride), and drive home. As I cruise past Samantha's shop, it somehow feels like she's still watching. Like she has eyes in the velvet drapes or something.

I park at my place and start lugging groceries in, making several trips like a peasant without arms made of octopus. I unpack everything and reward myself with chips and salsa. Obviously.

I wonder what Ryan's up to.

Right on cue, my phone chirps. I laugh. Wouldn't it be something if it *was* him?

But nope—it's Betty.

*"Hi, Fran! So update: bachelorette is next weekend! Piper planned it. I hope you're ready for some wine drinking!"*

I raise an eyebrow. Piper planned it? *Piper*? Interesting. She didn't reach out to ask for ideas, money, *anything*. Not even a meme.

I text Betty back, asking for the details, and she responds immediately—clearly vibrating with excitement over the whole wine-drenched ordeal.

Well then.

I guess I'm busy next weekend.

# EIGHTEEN

"This is going to be *lit*," Betty squeals, hopping out of my car.

I wince at her attempt to adopt new slang as I step out too, taking in the small, quaint cottage.

"This is cute," I smile.

Piper smirks. "Right? Figured you girls would love it."

As Betty and Miranda skip ahead to unlock the door, I gently pull Piper back.

"Hey, Piper?"

"What's up, doll?" she asks, catching her reflection in her compact mirror.

"I just wanted to ask—why didn't you reach out about booking this place or anything? I mean, you can't go wrong with wine tastings and a cozy cottage, but..." I trail off with a shrug.

Piper places a hand on my shoulder and gives me a pout, the kind that feels more rehearsed than sincere.

"Aw, Franny. I'm *so* sorry—I saw this deal and just *knew* it was what Betty wanted. And, well, being the maid of honor, I figured I'd jump on it. Must've slipped my mind to loop you in. Forgive me?"

Why does she always sound like a sorority president trying to win class president?

"Sure, Piper. Forgiven."

"Perf," she chirps, showing me exactly where Betty picked up the lingo. "Let's unpack, kay?"

"Kay," I mimic, matching her cheeriness with my best polite smile.

As I grab my suitcase, a thought hits me: even after all this personal growth, I'm allowed not to like someone. And I really don't like Piper. I also don't understand how she and Betty are friends—or how she ended up maid of honor in the first place. Did I miss something?

Inside, Betty's already twirling in the living room. I wave her down. "Uh, where am I sleeping?"

"Anywhere, babe," she says, accepting a glass from Miranda. "Wherever your heart desires!"

She's already drunk? How?

I head upstairs and find a small room with a double bed and a fuzzy white rug. It feels cozy enough. I toss my suitcase on the bed and unpack a few things into the dresser.

"Hot tub!" Piper's voice shrieks from below.

I keep my swimsuit out, just in case she's serious. When I head back down, Betty spins toward me, arms wide.

"Fran!" she beams.

"Yes, Betty?" I laugh, wrapping her in a hug.

"I'm so happy," she sighs, eyes glassy and heart clearly full.

I kiss her cheek. "You deserve to be."

"Seriously though...hot tub?" Piper calls out again.

Miranda, ever the voice of reason, gestures toward the fridge. "Maybe we should eat first. Then we can wine-and-soak."

"Great idea," I nod. "We definitely need something to soak up all the alcohol."

"Oh, Francine," Piper sighs dramatically. "You're totally going to be the mom of this weekend. Who worries about alcohol on a bachelorette?"

I stick my tongue out at her—the most polite way I can say *please shut up*. She has no idea how alcohol's affected my life before, and frankly, I'm not about to unpack it for her. Let her drink her calories and regret it later. I plan to remember this weekend, enjoy it, and sing loudly—*very* loudly—while Piper nurses her regrets from under a comforter.

I sip my water smugly.

We throw together some homemade pizzas, laughter and wine starting to swirl into the air. Piper pops open our first bottle—a crisp white—and Miranda hands me a glass just as my phone lights up on the counter. It's Ryan.

He asks what I'm up to, so I snap a photo of the four of us mid-giggle and text it along with an update. He replies with a parade of laughing emojis and a sweet *have the best time* message.

"Let's get naked!"

We all spin around to face Miranda, who turns bright red.

"Just kidding. Suits on, girls."

We head off to change. I slip into a comfy navy one-piece, just cheeky enough to feel cute but still functional. Piper waltzes out in a microscopic hot pink bikini—of course—and clucks her tongue at me.

"Oh, I *know* you've got a great body under there. Why hide it?"

I blush. "Not hiding anything. It's just... comfy."

"I can tell," she says with a knowing smirk, strutting down the stairs like she's on a runway.

*Eugh.*

I follow her down, and Piper tosses her towel into the air like it's a victory flag.

"Bubbly time!"

"I got it," Miranda says, holding up a bottle of champagne.

Piper scoffs. "I meant the *hot tub* bubbly, Miranda."

"Oops. Still not opening it though. Corks scare me."

She hands the bottle to Piper and steps back. Piper rolls her eyes and tosses her towel aside.

"I thought we were having wine," she mutters.

"I wanted champagne," Betty shrugs, adjusting her strappy purple bikini. "And what the bride wants, the bride gets."

Piper takes the bottle with exaggerated confidence. "It's just a cork. How hard can it be?"

She wrestles with it, muttering, twisting, grumbling. Nothing happens.

"What is with this stupid—"

**POP!**

The cork blasts her square in the forehead.

For a heartbeat, silence.

Then chaos.

Miranda faceplants onto the island, shaking with laughter. Betty slaps the counter over and over, tears streaking her cheeks. I double over, hands on my knees, gasping between fits of cackling.

That cork may as well have been Cupid's arrow straight to my serotonin.

Piper groans, rubbing the little pink welt on her forehead.

"Hardy har har. Glad I could be the clown of the weekend. That *hurt*."

She examines the mark in her phone camera, pouting. Betty finally catches her breath enough to speak. "I'm... I'm sorry, Pipe. It was just *so* cinematic. Like something out of a sketch comedy show."

"Yeah," Miranda nods, hoisting herself off the island. "Sorry we laughed. That's why I'm scared of opening champagne—it can be lethal."

Piper waves a dismissive hand. "No, it's fine. I can only imagine how ridiculous it looked. Let's hit the hot tub."

She pours us each a glass of bubbly, and we pile into the hot tub one by one. It's a little too cozy for four grown women, but we manage to squish in. Betty leans back against the jets and moans blissfully.

"Oh my god, I may never leave this tub."

"Same," Miranda sighs, carefully placing her glasses on the little table to her left before closing her eyes and humming contentedly.

"Speaking of humming, let's get some tunes going," I suggest.

Piper points a wet finger at me. "Smart!"

She lurches up out of the tub, butt sky-high, grunting as she reaches for her phone. "Okay... what are we feeling?"

"Dance party, obviously," Betty says, already bopping in place. Her goofy dancing turns the hot tub into a human wave pool.

We blast some throwback hits and sip our champagne way too fast. Honestly, it's been a surprisingly chill and fun night—aside from Piper being, well... Piper. When the water starts to feel more like soup than luxury, we all towel off.

"Wine tour tomorrow?" Betty asks, twisting her hair into a makeshift turban.

"You know it," Miranda grins, flopping onto the couch. "We've got some amazing wineries lined up. Just... please tell me there won't be strippers."

"There isn't," Piper groans. "Betty wanted to be a bore."

**Talk to Betty about Piper. She'll thank you.**

I glance at Betty, who rolls her eyes. I'd been debating whether to say anything—her friendships aren't my business—but apparently, the mystical antique has other ideas. As Piper and Miranda fall into another chat, I gently pull Betty aside and place my hands on her shoulders.

"Hey, Betty... are you okay?"

She blinks. "Why wouldn't I be?"

"It's just... Piper seems a little harsh. No filter. Doesn't really feel like someone you'd usually vibe with, you know?"

Betty shrugs. "I don't know. When I first met her, we just clicked. She brought a lot of energy to my life when I needed it. But... yeah. I do see what you mean. She's very... about herself."

We both glance over. Piper is waving her hands dramatically in Miranda's face about something or other.

"You're allowed to be friends with whoever you want," I say gently. "I just want to make sure you're surrounded by people who genuinely have your back."

"Like you?"

I wince. "Yes... now. I'm making up for it."

Betty gives a soft smile, then pulls me into a hug, the scent of her signature floral perfume wrapping around me.

"Thanks, Fran."

We crash about an hour later, the night wrapping up peacefully. I lie in bed, eyes tracing the wooden ceiling above me, noting the deep grains and the various little knots in the timber. I've come such a long way since that emotionally-fueled road trip to Dudsville—the day I met the figurine.

As sleep begins to pull me under, I catch a dark marking in the wood above me. An etching... shaped like an owl.

# Nineteen

The rest of the bachelorette was filled with giggles, wine, and flirting. To be clear, the flirting was courtesy of Piper—none of the rest of us. Miranda was committed to someone, I had Ryan, and Betty, of course, had Phil.

We said our goodbyes, and just as I was settling into the driver's seat for the long trek home, Betty ran over and hugged me one last time.

"I'm so lucky to have you as a friend," she said. "Don't forget to bring Ryan! See you in a week!"

Now, a week later, I'm standing in front of my mirror, sprucing myself up and getting ready to watch my best friend walk down the aisle. The last wedding I attended was my mother's—the one where I met Ryan. The contrast between my life then and now is monumental. And honestly? I wouldn't change a thing.

Piper walks into the room, her long blonde hair curled and bouncy.

"Oh, Fran, wow!"

I smile and take her in. "Same to you!"

"Right?" She smirks at her reflection beside mine. "Can you believe Betty is getting married?!"

"I can't," I say with a soft smile, "but I'm so happy for her."

"Girls?"

We both turn—and gasp.

Betty stands there glowing in her ball gown, glitter sparkling in her half-updo. Miranda, clearly responsible for the finished look, beams behind her.

"What do you think?" Betty asks, turning with a twirl, her full skirt following like a cloud of elegance.

"You are so gorgeous, it isn't fair!" Piper whines, rushing to hug her.

I follow, hugging her tightly. "Betty, you look perfect."

"Let's get you married!" Miranda claps, gently guiding her toward the ballroom doors for her big entrance.

The music swells. Piper squeaks, "It's time!"

I walk in first, scanning the crowd filled with unfamiliar faces. I spot Ryan and Betty's mom, both beaming. I smile as I take my place, watching Miranda sashay up the aisle, then Piper.

Betty's flower girl follows, enthusiastically flinging white petals everywhere—some even land on guests' laps. Everyone chuckles, clearly charmed, and her mother beams with pride as the little one takes her place.

Then everyone rises.

Betty appears, radiating joy as she walks down the aisle on her father's arm. Her eyes never leave Phil. I glance over to see Phil's eyes glistening as he watches her approach.

Betty winks at me, and I wink back as she reaches him, passing her bouquet to Piper.

"Here, take hers. I already have mine leaking on me," Piper whispers to Miranda, handing off the bouquet.

"And mine isn't?" Miranda mutters, but complies.

I shake my head slightly—Piper never fails to be, well, Piper.

The vows begin. The ring exchange. The tenderness of it all hits me hard. I can't help but reflect on what could've been—how this almost was me. But with the wrong guy.

I imagine the absurdity of saying vows to Greg, only for him to interrupt with a raised finger. A murmur ripples through the guests as he pulls out a massive bottle of beer, chugs it without pausing for breath, then wipes his mouth with his tuxedo sleeve before belching like it's his wedding gift to the crowd. It's excessive. It's absurd. It's Greg.

I snap back to the present as the room erupts into applause and cheers.

I join in, smiling, clapping along with everyone else. I glance at Ryan—he's smiling too, a wide, proud grin on his face. He winks at me. I blush, returning the gesture.

And just like that, the image shifts. This time it's me and Ryan, sober and grounded, staring into each other's eyes as we say our vows. The kiss is cinematic.

I follow the newlyweds down the aisle, feeling Ryan's hand gently brush my shoulder as I pass him.

"How romantic," Miranda squeaks, watching Betty and Phil disappear around the corner, giggling like teenagers.

"Super romantic," Piper nods, reclaiming her bouquet. "Thanks, doll!"

We mingle in the fading afterglow while guests file out of the ceremony space so the staff can flip it into full-blown reception mode.

"You are beautiful," Ryan says emphatically, taking my hands. "Have I told you that yet?"

I tap my chin, feigning deep thought. "Hmm, it might be slightly overdue."

Miranda catches Ryan's enthusiasm and throws me a dramatic thumbs-up behind his back. I smile as Ryan kisses me softly.

"Pictures!" Betty calls, waving us over.

"Duty calls," I say, planting a kiss on Ryan's nose. "You good here?"

He plucks a baguette off a passing tray like it's the love of his life. "With these treats? Hell yeah."

Piper loops her arm through mine and yanks me toward the chaos of post-ceremony photography. We're shuffled into position after position, the photographer calling out directions like we're on a bridal fashion runway.

"I'm starved," Piper groans, pausing mid-adjustment to hike up her cleavage.

"We all are, princess," Miranda mutters, her tone laced with dry contempt.

I blink. Did Miranda just snap?

"Excuse me," Piper whirls on her. "I don't appreciate your tone."

Betty returns from her solo shots just in time for the storm to roll in. I step between them.

"Ladies," I say firmly. "This is Betty's day. Can we hit pause on the catfight?"

Piper rolls her eyes like it's a sport, while Miranda nods, visibly checking herself.

"You're right, Fran," Miranda says.

Satisfied for now, we all refocus as we're ushered back to line up for our grand entrance.

Kason, Phil's best man and apparent professional flirt, sidles up beside me and slows to match my pace.

"Fran, is it?"

"It is."

"That color suits you perfectly," he says, gesturing to my blue dress like he's appraising rare fabric. "Have you come with anyone?"

Wow. Wasting zero time.

"Actually, yes. I have."

His grin falters. "Ah, how unfortunate."

I tilt my head toward Piper, who's fluffing herself like a peacock in a wind tunnel. "Go for her."

**You beat me to it! Looks like you're getting the hang of this!**

I smirk, feeling the smug satisfaction of outmaneuvering a magical antique in matchmaking.

"Piper?" Kason blinks. "You think she'd go for me?"

"Doesn't hurt to try," I shrug.

He nods, intrigued, and wanders off in her direction as I smooth my dress. The doors swing open and the DJ starts announcing us one by one. I bust a few awkward moves on my way to the front, feeling half like a guest and half like a backup dancer in a wedding-themed music video.

I slide into my seat near the head table, eyeing the regal layout. A king's table... I kind of love that idea.

Betty and Phil enter to a predictable party anthem, heading straight into their first dance. The lights dim. Smoke billows out from nowhere like a magician's trick. It's over-the-top and a little corny—and I'm completely charmed.

The room claps as guests take their seats, smiles all around.

Across from me, Piper grins wide, clapping. "This night is gonna be amazing. That Kason guy totally has the hots for me, and my speech is going to *slap*."

"S-slap?" I echo.

She rolls her eyes. "Oh, come on, Fran. Get with the times. It means it'll be amazing."

"Then why don't you just *say* that?" Miranda mutters, taking a sip of her water.

Soon, the food arrives, a welcome distraction. I dig in happily, casting a glance over at Ryan's table. He's chatting with the woman next to him, handing her a cup. I clock it, then remind myself: it's water, not a wedding proposal.

"This is *delicious*," Miranda nods, clearing her plate like she hasn't eaten in days. I nod in agreement and polish mine off not long after.

Piper suddenly pops up, smoothing her dress with a dramatic flair. "Alright, girls. It's my time to shine."

"Should we be worried?" Miranda asks, grimacing.

"I'll do damage control," I sigh, hands already halfway in the air.

Piper taps the mic—hard. The sharp feedback screech makes every guest recoil. Undeterred, she grins at the crowd like she just hit the first note of her one-woman show.

"Hi, everyone! So sweet of you to come out for our dear Betty and Phil!"

She launches into her speech like it's an audition reel for *Real Housewives: Wedding Edition*.

"For those who know me, I'm Piper. I met Betty way back in university. She was a lost little lamb with glasses and, like, *questionable* fashion. I knew she had potential though—and I basically treated her like my real-life Barbie doll! But then we actually became true friends."

I glance toward the head table. Betty's smile has gone stiff. Phil looks like he's trying not to breathe.

"And okay, I was a bit unsure about Phil at first—who *chooses their guy friends over their girlfriend every weekend*, am I right?" She laughs, apparently forgetting this is *not* a roast.

Someone coughs in the audience. A napkin drops. It's the loudest sound in the room.

"Anyway, guess it all worked out, huh?" Piper says brightly. "Now that you're *married*, maybe you'll actually spend time together!"

Betty's eyes glisten. Phil shifts uncomfortably. Piper, oblivious, powers through.

"She's always been sweet to me. I had a lot of issues with my body—like, *looking this good isn't easy*—and she accepted me for who I was…" Her voice cracks, and she dabs a tear. "Ugh, my life is so hard."

Betty drops her gaze to her lap, shoulders trembling. I shoot up from my seat.

Piper blinks at me and cocks a brow. "Listen, I know it must suck not being the maid of honour, but last I checked, you don't get a speech. Sit down. I'm not done yet."

***Tread lightly here.***

The magical voice in my head cuts through the white-hot burn of embarrassment and rage. I take a steadying breath.

"No," I say calmly, "but you *are* done, Piper."

She frowns, confused.

"What?"

Phil is glaring. Betty won't even look up. The silence is vacuum-sealed.

"I don't understand. What's wrong?"

"Everything," Betty says suddenly, her voice tight and shaky. "*Everything*, Piper!"

She bolts up from her seat, Phil stumbling after her.

"Wait—babe!"

But she's gone. The doors swing closed behind her like punctuation.

Gasps ripple through the room. Piper shrugs at the audience, baffled.

"What *is* the issue?"

I guide her firmly away from the mic and lower my voice.

"The issue," I say, "is that you just humiliated your *best friend* on her wedding day. You insulted Phil, made fun of Betty's past, and then—somehow—made it all about *you*. Again."

Piper blinks like she's hearing an alien language.

"You need to open your eyes," I continue, "or one day you're going to look around and realize you've got no one left."

She stutters, but I don't stay to hear it. Behind me, I hear Miranda gracefully slide into cleanup mode.

"Sorry, guests! We'll be back up and running in no time—enjoy the food!"

I round the corner and find Betty seated on a plush chair, her voluminous dress spilling around her like a snow globe that cracked open. Her makeup—once perfect—is smudged at the edges, but not ruined. She must've stopped herself just in time.

She sniffs, offering a watery shrug. "What's a wedding without a little drama, right?"

I kneel in front of her, frowning as I hand over a napkin. She dabs her cheeks delicately.

"Couldn't keep ruining my makeup," she murmurs.

*Called it.*

"Betty," I start gently, "that must not have been easy to hear."

She blows her nose with a honk. "No. It wasn't. It was mortifying. What the hell is wrong with me? Why did I stay friends with her for so long?"

I lower myself onto the cool marble floor beside her. "Because sometimes, it's hard to see someone clearly when they've been in your life forever. And it's even harder to cut them out."

She sniffles again, eyes brimming. "You even warned me at the bachelorette. Why didn't I see it sooner? She's selfish. She's rude. And now she's *ruined my wedding*. Poor Phil…"

I take her hands in mine. "This isn't your fault. Don't blame yourself for having a big heart. But now that you *do* see it, we can deal with her properly. Want me to make sure she goes home?"

"Betty?"

Phil's voice cuts in softly. He stands a few feet away, fingers interlocked tightly, anxiety painted across his face.

"You okay, babe?"

Betty nods slowly. "I think so. Phil, I'm *so* sorry she spoke about you that way. I swear, the blindfold's off. Fully off."

I rise, giving Phil a nod. "I'll leave you two. I'm really sorry this happened."

Phil hugs me tight. "You have *nothing* to apologize for, okay? Thank you for always being there for her. Honestly, you should've been the maid of honour," he adds with a wink.

I smile and slip back toward the ballroom, ready to assess the social fallout.

Some guests are crowding the open bar, cocktails in hand. Others are murmuring quietly, eyes drifting toward Piper and Kason, who are huddled off to the side.

Piper is in full meltdown, tears streaming down her cheeks as she sniffs and clutches a cocktail napkin like it's a lifeline.

"Oh my God," she cries, "Kason is so right. I've been *an awful* friend."

*Wait— Kason* got through to her? What did he say—read from a therapy manual while juggling her emotional baggage?

"I'm glad someone finally reached you," I say, voice calm but firm. "I hope you'll apologize. And change. Because if you don't… I won't let Betty be hurt by you again."

Piper nods feverishly, wiping her nose on her arm like a first-grade disaster.

"I—I know. I knew I met Kason for a reason. I'm gonna go find Betty."

She wanders off, guests pretending not to watch her, eyes darting away like they weren't *just* eating up the drama. I cross my arms and eye Kason.

"What exactly did you say to her?"

In my peripheral vision, I see Ryan excusing himself from his table, heading over as Kason answers, "I just gave it to her straight. She was being a selfish, vain girl—and she needed to smarten up."

I raise an eyebrow so sharp it could slice fondant. *Really?* That's all it took? Meanwhile, *I* got a magical warning to tread lightly. What gives, figurine?

Ryan touches my arm gently, concern etched across his features. "Everything okay?"

I run my fingers through my helmet of hairspray and bridal party stress. "Yeah. I expected Piper to say something ridiculous—I just didn't expect *that*. I feel so bad for Betty."

Ryan shrugs. "I feel like every wedding needs one catastrophic speech. It's tradition at this point."

Kason slides his hands into his pockets and looks down at the floor, probably reflecting on the emotional demolition derby we just witnessed. I realize I should introduce them.

"Ryan, this is Kason—Phil's best friend. Kason, this is Ryan—my boyfriend."

"Ah, the infamous boyfriend," Kason says with a sly grin.

Ryan raises an eyebrow, and I can *feel* the confusion in his body language. He probably clocked that I only met Kason, like, *three hours ago*, so the 'infamous' comment might've sent his brain into a spin cycle.

"Oh yes," Ryan deadpans, pulling me closer. "I am quite infamous."

He gives Kason a nod that basically says *'thanks for the weird energy'* and turns to me. "Now, if you'll excuse us, we should check on the newlyweds."

Oh, the testosterone is palpable. You could wring it out and bottle it as cologne.

Just then, a woman with enough perfume to fumigate a small city approaches from behind. "Oh, there they are!"

We all glance over to see Betty and Phil reenter the ballroom. Polite applause follows them like a light golf clap wave. Piper trails behind them, clearly trying not to look like she's doing the walk of shame in heels.

I wave Betty over. "So… did Piper find you?"

"Yeah," Betty mutters, rolling her eyes. "She apologized. Tears and all. I just… I don't know what's real and what's fake with her anymore. Let's just sit and get through dinner."

Ryan kisses my forehead and murmurs, "See you on the dance floor."

I sink into my seat as Piper plops down across from me. I avoid her gaze and take a heroic gulp of my wine.

*Weddings are drama central.*

My brain floats away to the fantasy of my own wedding—destination style. Minimal guests. Maximum views. The venue does the setup. There's no drama, no distractions, just vows on the beach and a seamless slide into honeymoon mode.

Why doesn't everyone do it that way? No reception speeches. No rogue maids of honour. Just breezy, barefoot perfection.

"Fran?"

I return to the table to find Piper fidgeting, clearly trying to catch my attention.

"Yes, Piper?" I ask coolly.

"I… I just wanted to say how sorry I am. For everything. To you… and Miranda."

Miranda sighs, swirling her wine in her glass like she's trying to find patience at the bottom.

I nod slowly. "I just hope you mean that. I hope you *actually* understand how inappropriate that was—and how selfish you've been through this whole process."

Piper stares down at her perfectly manicured nails. "Yeah… I'm starting to see that now."

I finish my meal in silence, sliding my plate to the side for pick-up just as Kason steps up to the mic. He adjusts it slightly and surveys the room.

"Well," he starts, grinning, "that's a pretty easy act to follow."

Nervous giggles ripple through the guests. Piper's glare could probably melt silverware.

"So, Phil has been my best friend for as long as I can remember. You know those movies where two kids grow up on the same street and cause mayhem together? That was us. Always out too late, always getting yelled at by our moms, and always thinking it was worth it."

Phil chuckles and plants a sweet kiss on Betty's cheek.

Kason continues, "I knew Betty was the one for Phil almost right away. She's got the same adventurous, kind, let's-do-something-insane spirit we thrived on. And she doesn't just love him—she *supports* him. Like really supports him. That's rare. That's magic. And Betty, for that... I love you too."

A collective *aww* hums through the room.

"I wish you two nothing but the best," Kason says warmly. "And hey, I wouldn't mind being godfather to your future little rascals."

Betty sticks her tongue out at him and the room erupts into laughter and applause—relief practically steaming off the crowd. *That's* the speech we needed.

I shoot Kason a grateful wink as he pats Piper once—more gentle this time—and returns to our table.

Dinner wraps up and the music kicks into gear, leading us into the predictable but cherished chaos of dancing.

I walk over to Ryan, placing both hands on his shoulders. "I do believe we've been apart long enough tonight, wouldn't you think?"

He turns with a smile, taking my hand. "Couldn't agree more."

I gesture toward the dance floor, now occupied by tipsy guests with no shame. "Want to dance?"

"With you? Always."

I guide him to the edge of the floor, the lights casting playful patterns across his face. We move together easily, like we've always danced like this—close, warm, and entirely absorbed in one another.

"You're beautiful, Fran," Ryan whispers, his lips brushing the shell of my ear.

"And you," I whisper back, heart swelling.

He presses closer, the pulse of the music syncing with mine. Lights swirl around us in a blur of color. He tucks a sweaty strand of hair behind my ear and I lean in, breath caught in my throat.

This. This is what life should feel like—letting go with someone you love, under a kaleidoscope sky of possibility.

"I love you," I say.

"I love you too," he replies without hesitation.

We kiss.

It's electric. Grounding. The kind of kiss that makes the universe pause in admiration. His thumb strokes the side of my neck and I shiver, bliss rippling through me.

**Perfect, Fran. Perfect.**

The figurine's voice returns like silk on skin.

*You may have thought this was lust... but it's the opposite. Surprise. You're about to end your journey with me—but don't fret. Your true journey is only just beginning.*

The words swirl in my head, echoing with every slow turn and beat drop. I think of the sins I supposedly committed under her watch. Were they sins… or lessons dressed in rebellion?

I don't have time to unpack the philosophy. Ryan spins me, pulling me back into the moment. And I go willingly—smiling wider than I have in years.

# TWENTY

The morning held promise—a beautiful day with opportunities for growth tucked into every sunbeam. I opened my eyes from a peaceful slumber as birds passed their melodies from beak to breeze, filling my room with a gentle soundtrack. Stretching at the edge of the bed, I watched sunlight flicker on the wall in front of me, occasionally brushing my pajamas in soft kisses before disappearing behind shy clouds. But even in hiding, the sun made its intention clear: today, it would shine.

    I felt movement behind me and turned to see Ryan stirring. His messy brunette hair gave him the look of a teenager after an all-nighter—equal parts chaotic and charming. I know, specific.

But it's true. He rubbed his eyes, then ran a hand over his quickly growing stubble. I've always loved stubble—not the full-blown mountain-man beard and not the barely-there kind. This. This was perfect stubble on the perfect man.

"Way to stare," Ryan muttered with a sleepy grin, pulling me out of my very serious stubble admiration session.

"Why do you look so tired?" I asked, choosing to dodge the accusation entirely. He sat up, letting his hair flop dramatically against the headboard.

"Could be the fact that someone couldn't keep their hands off me last night."

I snorted and launched a pillow at his face. "You wish, buddy."

"I do, in fact," he said, and before I could escape, he pulled me back into bed. I squealed, smacking his arms in playful protest. But let's be honest—those biceps? I wasn't going anywhere until he let me.

"So," he began, as I mentally transitioned to what we'd eat for breakfast. It was a perfect Sunday morning, a few weeks after Betty's wedding. She'd be home from her luxurious French Polynesian honeymoon tomorrow.

"Uh oh," I teased, poking his side.

"I was wondering if you wanted to have dinner with me tonight," he said, suddenly serious enough to catch my attention.

"Of course! Any occasion?"

"Not really. I just feel like we haven't had a romantic night out in a while—just the two of us. What do you think?"

"I think… let's do it." I smiled. "Now—what do *you* want for breakfast?"

He yawned, stretching like a cat, arms reaching for the ceiling. "You."

I rolled my eyes. "Okay, I see we're going to be difficult. I'll figure it out."

Throwing on track pants and a tee, I padded downstairs to the kitchen, mentally shelving my plan to visit Samantha at the antique shop. After the figurine gave me that cryptic little clue a few weeks back, I'd been meaning to stop by. But between a hectic work schedule and Ryan slowly moving in—yup, he officially agreed last week to start living here—there just hadn't been time. He said he was outgrowing his place anyway and loved the vibe of this town. It's been exciting, to say the least.

I grabbed the pancake mix and other essentials from the cupboard just as Ryan wandered in, scratching his head like a cartoon character waking up on a Saturday morning.

"Ooh, pancakes!" His eyes lit up at the sight of the box.

I laughed. "Yeah, it definitely feels like a pancake kind of day."

"Need any help?"

I waved him off with the spatula, "I'm good. Just set the table, please."

We were a cute little family unit in my cute little home in Dudsville—finally content. We sat down in front of a pancake mountain, and Ryan laughed at the almost comical display.

"Wow, Fran, are you surprising me with a get-together?"

"No," I chuckled, "I *always* accidentally make too much, even when I follow the directions."

"Lucky for you, I'm a hungry man," Ryan replied, diving into a plate stacked with three. I smirked and grabbed two for myself, drowning them in thick maple syrup.

"You know what would make these perfect?" Ryan tapped his fork against the plate with mock seriousness. "Whipped cream. Next time, we need whipped cream."

I lobbed a strawberry at him. "At least there's fruit for your health. Now eat!"

The rest of the day rolled by with the same playful energy—us being goofy, lounging, teasing, and loving around the house. But as the sun began its slow descent, painting the sky with sleepy golds and oranges, I started getting ready for our date.

I curled my red hair. I kept my makeup natural but elevated: long lashes, a soft pink stain on my lips, and just enough contour to feel like I had cheekbones worthy of a magazine spread. I slipped into a sleek blue dress and made my way downstairs.

Ryan was already waiting, dressed in a fitted button-down and a grey blazer with matching pants.

"Wow, Francine," he breathed, eyes raking from my head to my heels, "you look incredible."

The air practically crackled with sexual tension. We always had that—an undeniable passion and connection. Two lost souls who, somehow, finally collided in the right place at the right time.

"You clean up pretty nice yourself," I replied, sliding into my heels.

There was something in the air. This didn't feel like *just* a date.

He led me to his car and buckled into the driver's seat. "Excited for some good food?"

I raised a hand. "When am I not?"

"Touché," he chuckled, starting the car.

As we drove out of Dudsville and closer to the city I once shared with Greg, my thoughts drifted—briefly and involuntarily. I wondered where Greg was. Probably still knee-deep in alcohol and fresh excuses. Who was I kidding? Of course he was.

A Phil Collins classic came on the radio, and Ryan sighed contentedly. "Man, this guy never gets old."

"He really doesn't," I agreed, letting the music fill the comfortable silence between us.

Soon, Ryan found a parking spot on a narrow street and executed a perfect parallel park.

"Very impressive," I noted as I unbuckled. "Most people wouldn't dare parallel park on a date. Too risky for the ego."

"I'm very impressive, Francine," he winked, taking my hand.

We walked up a small staircase and through an old building door, stepping into a modest lobby. He pressed the button for the elevator.

"Oh, this is it, isn't it?" I teased. "This is where you murder me. I *knew* this was too good to be true."

Ryan just pulled me close, kissing the top of my head.

As we stepped into the elevator and the doors closed behind us, I mused aloud, "You know, I've never actually heard elevator music. It's such a cliché in movies, but I don't think it really exists."

"I've heard it once," Ryan smiled, "just once."

The doors opened, revealing a stunning rooftop bar and restaurant. It was completely empty— except for one smiling hostess. The view was breathtaking: city lights twinkling like tiny dancers, stars scattered across the sky like freckles. Like *my* freckles.

"Welcome, Ryan," the hostess greeted him, then turned to me. "And welcome to *The Rise*. Let me show you to your table."

She guided us to what was very clearly the best seat in the house, overlooking the glittering skyline.

"Uh… where is everyone?" I asked, scanning the empty space.

"I booked the whole place for us," Ryan said casually, settling into his seat with a proud grin.

My jaw dropped. Before I could say anything, he turned to the hostess and added, "Can you bring us your finest bottle of white?"

"Of course! Your server will be with you shortly."

As she skipped away, I arched a brow. "Okay, mister. *What* is this?"

"What's what?" he asks, feigning innocence. "I have no idea what you're talking about."

"Sure you don't," I roll my eyes. "This is quite the last-minute date."

He just grins, saying nothing more.

Our server returns with the wine Ryan requested and nods at him—a silent confirmation that he'll sample it first. Ryan swirls the wine in his glass like a true connoisseur, takes a small sip, then smiles. "This is perfect."

She pours wine into my glass, and I join him on this little tasting journey, savoring how the different notes dance on my tongue.

"This is great," I confirm, loving whites way more than reds. We chat about how much we enjoyed the day, how relaxing it was. Ryan rubs his foot against my leg, and I feel the heat sparking between us again.

"So, Francine. You're happy with me, right?"

I nod, smiling warmly. "I couldn't be happier, Ryan. You've really opened my eyes to what true happiness and growth in a relationship feels like. I honestly can't thank you enough."

Ryan laughs that famous deep, beautiful laugh. "You don't need to thank me for treating you right. People who've been wronged in the past say things like, 'Thank you for being amazing to me. I don't deserve you.' But really? Love and respect should just be the *foundation* of any relationship. It should just... happen."

I take another sip of my wine, nodding. "You're right. But I can still thank you for being an amazing human, Ryan."

He winks. "I'll take it."

We peruse the menu, and my old anxiety about eating messy food in front of him fades away. I'd always thought the first few dates meant avoiding wings and sushi—things that might make you look imperfect. You had to show grace and perfection. But as I pick a saucy pasta dish, ready to wear some sauce on my chin with pride, I know real perfection is being yourself in front of people who are also perfectly imperfect. Sauce on your chin or cheeks, be damned.

"I feel like tonight I'll regret not ordering what you got," Ryan laughs, debating his steak decision.

"You can't go wrong with steak," I say.

"I've had many bad orders come back," he sighs. "But I believe in these guys."

Ryan takes my hands, smiling softly. "You know you're really important to me, right?"

Okay, weird vibes incoming. "Of course, Ryan. Why are you being so sappy all of a sudden?"

He shrugs. "No reason. I just feel like I don't tell you these things enough."

Our food arrives about five minutes later. I immediately approve of my choice—the red sauce coating the soft pasta, the perfect scatter of fresh basil.

"I'm definitely stealing a bite," Ryan smirks.

I pucker my lips. "I'll think about it."

We dig in. Ryan's steak is cooked perfectly. My pasta melts in my mouth, the blend of cheeses rich and heavenly. Thank God I'm not lactose intolerant—though, honestly, the lactose intolerant folks I know still sneak dairy whenever they can. I scoop up the remaining sauce after letting Ryan savor it with a piece of bread, then lean back, completely content.

Ryan pours the last bit of wine from the bottle into my glass. I sigh happily. "This has been an amazing dinner. Thank you for bringing me here. It feels a bit odd that no one else is around, but that private vibe is perfect."

"I'm glad you're enjoying yourself," Ryan says, reaching for his water, the ice now half-melted. I do the same, feeling the wine start to play little games in my head.

"Now for dessert," Ryan claps his hands, eyes scanning for the server. I rub my belly like I'm already full to the brim. "I don't think I can. That pasta was very filling."

"Too bad," he says simply.

I raise an eyebrow, watching Ryan's face—a bit lost in thought, his body tense, not his usual relaxed self. His foot starts tapping nervously, eyes darting around as if willing the server to appear out of thin air.

"Ryan, you okay?"

He nods quickly and raises his hand as the server emerges from the kitchen. "Excuse me? We'd like dessert now."

She smiles and takes away our plates. "Dinner good?"

"Excellent, thanks," Ryan answers, foot still tapping.

My phone buzzes on the table. I glance down—a message from Betty.

*Fran! What you doing right now? We need to talk.*

"Everything okay?" I ask Ryan, showing him the message.

"Oh, yeah. Betty wants to talk."

"You can call her if you want."

"No, it's fine. I'll let her know I'm at dinner and call later." I shoot off a quick reply. She texts back with a simple *okay* just as the kitchen door swings open again. This time the server arrives with a bottle of champagne and two flutes.

"We'll bring dessert out in a moment. Enjoy this champagne for now," she says, handing us the glasses.

Ryan raises his glass with a grin. I chuckle, "My gosh, you're going to have to carry me home."

He just waits, seriously, and I clink my glass against his, taking a long sip of the bubbly liquid.

Then I spot something glinting at the bottom of my flute. "Hey, something's in the bottom of my glass."

"What is it?" Ryan leans in.

I dip a finger in, muttering, "I should've washed my hands before this…" and pull out—

A huge, sparkling solitaire ring.

I stare between the ring and Ryan. He stands and moves to my side of the table.

"Ryan…" I start, breath catching.

He kneels. "Francine. You are an incredible woman, inside and out. Since meeting you at your mom's wedding, I've seen you grow into someone even more amazing. I can't imagine my life without you. Will you make me the happiest man alive and marry me?"

My throat tightens. Am I ready? So soon?

**Francine. Yes.**

My heart pounding, I nod over and over, "Yes, Ryan. Yes!"

He exhales the breath he'd been holding and slides the ring onto my left hand.

"Oh my God." I stand and kiss him, our hearts syncing, our tongues dancing.

Ryan brushes a thumb across my cheek, catching my tears silently spilling down. "I'm so happy you said yes."

"I'm so happy you asked," I whisper, gazing into his perfect eyes flecked with gold, the smile lines that deepen when he grins wide, and those big ears that wiggle with his smile. This man—he's perfect. This man is mine.

"Congratulations!" The server returns, pausing as she notices the ring. "Wait…congratulations are in order, right?"

I laugh, lifting my hand. "Yes."

She breathes a relieved sigh. "Awesome! Here's your dessert, loves!"

The server sets a rich cheesecake between us, "Congratulations" scrawled across the top in elegant chocolate script. We both slide back into our seats, hearts still buzzing.

I wipe at my eyes again. "Man, the tears won't stop coming."

Ryan scoops a generous bite onto his spoon and offers it to me. "As long as they're happy tears. You deserve the best, Francine."

I take the bite, letting the velvety sweetness melt on my tongue. And for the first time in a long time, I start to believe that. That maybe… I really am in a good place. Surrounded by love. Grounded in joy.

*Thank you for the guidance, woman of sin.*

**You're welcome.**

Outside, the warm city air greets us, brushing my hair across my cheeks like a gentle encore to the evening. My cheeks are still flushed from the surprise, and now, the cheesecake.

"Give me a sec," I say to Ryan, reaching for my phone. "Let me call Betty real quick."

It rings. And rings. I'm just about to pocket it when it vibrates again—FaceTime. I answer, and Betty's face fills the screen, camera too close like always.

"Hey girl! Where you at?"

"I just finished dinner with Ryan. Listen... I have news. But you go first."

"Okay!" she squeaks, disappearing off-screen for a second. I hear some muffled movement before she reappears, holding up a pregnancy test like it's a golden ticket. "I'm pregnant!"

My jaw drops, "Betty! That's amazing! Congrats to you and Phil!"

"Thanks, girl! It still feels unreal. Anyway, what's your news?"

"I don't want to take away from your moment. Mine can wait!"

"Fran," she says with a classic Betty eye-roll. "Tell. Me."

I exhale, glancing over at Ryan who's perched on a bench nearby, flashing me that soft, proud smile. "Okay... Ryan took me to this rooftop restaurant downtown. It was private, beautiful. Dinner was amazing and then... he proposed."

"WHAT?!" Betty screeches so loud I'm pretty sure we just startled a pigeon somewhere in Venice.

I grin, cheeks already hurting. "Yep. You heard me."

"You said yes, right? *Right?*"

"Of course I did."

She claps wildly, calling offscreen, "Phil! Ryan proposed!"

A faint "Congrats!" echoes in the background.

I show her the ring and she clutches her chest like she's going to cry. "Oh, Fran. You don't even know how happy I am for you. When you were with Greg, it was like he sucked the light out of you. I didn't know how to help... or what to say."

I nod, heart full. "I know. I felt so lost. He made me pull away from everyone I loved. But I woke up. And now I'm... exactly where I'm supposed to be."

Ryan walks over as I wave him into the frame.

"Hey, Betty!" he smiles. "Ready to be a bridesmaid?"

"*Maid of honour,* actually," she grins back. "Congrats, Ryan."

"Of course," I say, resting my head against him. "Congrats again on the pregnancy. Let us know if you need anything."

We sign off, and Ryan pulls me into his arms, warm and solid.

"What an evening," he murmurs.

"What an evening," I echo, as we take the long way back to the car—hand in hand, letting the city noise hum around us, our futures unfolding under the lights.

# Twenty-One

I take a deep breath, halting as my hand wraps around the handle of *Granny's Treasures*. This is it—the moment I've been waiting for all these months. Today is the day I get answers.

I think back to earlier this morning, Ryan heading out to work, telling me he'd be back later. As I stood in the kitchen wondering what to do with my day, that familiar, soft voice echoed in my mind:

*It's time, Francine. Take me back home, and you will receive all the answers.*

My heart raced. I grabbed her, my purse, and bolted to the car—only to forget my keys. *Shit, my keys!* I doubled back, snatched them from the counter, and drove here as safely—but quickly—as I could. Now I'm parked outside, staring at the door. Ready for clarity. Ready for truth.

I step inside. The bell jingles above me, and Samantha appears from the back, eyes twinkling. "Ah, Francine!" she says warmly, coming in for a hug.

"Hi, Samantha," I reply, nerves buzzing beneath my skin. "So... the woman of sin told me this morning to come here. She said it's time to return her and receive the answers."

My chest tightens. What if she doesn't believe me? What if she thinks I'm crazy?

But Samantha just beams. "Ah, yes. I had a feeling today was the day. Here—let me have her."

I hand over the figurine, almost reverently. Samantha smiles down at it. "Isn't she just fantastic?"

I nod, voice quiet. "She's helped me become the best version of myself. I can't thank her—or you—enough."

Without another word, Samantha walks to the front and flips the sign to *Closed*. She gestures for me to follow her again into the back room—the one with all the beautiful wooden furniture. I remember being here last time, sipping tea and collecting even more confusion. But not today.

Today is for answers.

She points to the same cozy seat. "Please—get comfortable. Make yourself at home."

That phrase feels weighty. Like it carries a hidden meaning. Still, I sit, the familiarity grounding me.

"Would you like a hot beverage?" she asks, gesturing to the same kettle.

"Please. It's a bit chilly out," I reply, grateful for anything to keep my hands busy while my mind races ahead.

She nods and busies herself with the tea. "Where's your husband?" I ask casually.

"Out and about," she says. "Always hunting for new antiques."

A few minutes later, she hands me a steaming mug and settles into the chair across from me, blowing gently on her own tea. I hold the cup close, savoring its warmth.

"Patience is hard, isn't it?" she says knowingly.

I let out a breath and laugh, caught. "Yes. I'm sorry if I'm being rude."

"You're not being rude, dear. I understand the urgency. After being in the dark for so long, it's only natural to crave answers. I was in your position once too, you know."

I recall her saying she met her husband thanks to the antique. Which can only mean...

"She guided you too, didn't she?"

Samantha nods, wrapping her hands around her mug. I mimic her, the warmth soothing my fingers. "She did. And like you, there were moments when her requests confused me. They felt... random."

I nod, remembering. "Yes—like telling me to go to the casino to win money."

"Exactly," she says with a chuckle. Then she leans forward. "So... are you ready?"

"Yes."

She nods solemnly. "First, tell me what you've learned. From the very beginning—what has the woman of sin taught you?"

I inhale deeply, letting the journey play like a movie reel in my mind—from the day I brought her home to a drunken Greg, to this morning's whisper in my mind.

"I've learned a lot," I say slowly, thoughtfully. "I've learned that you should never settle for someone who dims your light. I've learned that your happiness should never be second—or last.

I've learned that true love… loves you back. I've learned not to push away the people who matter. And I've learned to live life fully—no matter how messy or uncertain."

I finish speaking, feeling like I could keep going forever. The words had poured out of me like a release I didn't know I needed.

Samantha takes her first sip of tea, closing her eyes briefly before opening them again, her gaze settling on me with a weight that makes me sit a little straighter.

"That's perfect, Francine. Just perfect." She sets her mug down gently. "Now… to start. I lied to you."

What?

My brow furrows. *What could she have possibly lied about?* My heart picks up speed, mind racing through every memory of her, every interaction. Was this all fake?

"H-how?" I ask, voice tight. "What did you lie about?"

She smiles softly. "Her name. It isn't the woman of sin."

I blink. "It… it's not?!"

That one takes me completely off guard. "There were so many times I actually wondered why she was called *sin*. It didn't seem like I was, well… sinning."

"That's because you weren't," Samantha confirms, nodding gently. "Her real name is *The Woman of Destination.*"

I sit with that, letting it tumble around in my head. My eyes widen slowly as I work through the name—*destination* does have *sin* right in the middle, broken up by the 'T'. Sin in the name, but not the purpose.

"*Sin* is in the name," I murmur.

Samantha smiles proudly. "Great job, Fran. That's exactly it. Now... let me walk you through some history."

I take my first sip of tea, letting the warmth tether me to this surreal moment. This is insane. This is trickery. This is... incredible.

"This figurine dates back to 898 BC," Samantha begins. "All we know is that it was created by someone with powerful magical abilities—someone who wanted to help others in the way she wished someone had helped her. Over centuries, the Woman of Destination has traveled the world, finding those who are lost and guiding them back to themselves. You, my dear, are the most recent."

I listen, captivated, as she continues.

"I was once like you. I stumbled into this shop, feeling directionless. I didn't know what step to take next—or if I even *should* take another step. A wise woman, the previous owner, emerged from the back and guided me, just like I've guided you. She didn't give me answers. She nudged me, challenged me, waited until I'd grown into the person I needed to be. And when the time was right, I was brought up to speed."

She leans forward slightly, her eyes gleaming with something deeper—something ancient. "You're probably wondering: why would this ancient artifact help people, asking for nothing in return?"

I let out a small laugh. "That's *exactly* what I've been wondering. I kept waiting for the catch."

Samantha lifts her mug in a toast. "There is a catch... sort of. But I doubt you'll be opposed to it. I certainly wasn't."

I narrow my eyes playfully. "Okay, what is it?"

She takes another slow sip, letting the mystery hang deliciously in the air. "You're going to take over. From me."

"Take over... what?"

She gestures around us. "This. The shop. The mission."

My jaw drops. "W–what? Really?"

She nods calmly. "Yes. You've been chosen. When someone completes their journey, they become the guide for the next soul. You'll take over the store as my time here ends. You'll be the next caretaker. The one to help the next lost soul find their path."

I stare at her, stunned. "That's... wow."

"Indeed," she says, eyes twinkling. "So—are you up for the challenge?"

I take another sip, the tea grounding me in this new reality. I lean back in my chair—*my* chair now—and smile. "Yes. I think I am."

"Perfect!" Samantha claps her hands in delight. "How wonderful this has come full circle. So satisfying."

We finish our tea in comfortable silence, the kind that wraps around you like a warm blanket. But one last question keeps tugging at the back of my mind.

"Sorry, but... you said I wasn't sinning. And yet, throughout the journey, the figurine mentioned lust, greed, things like that. So I'm a little confused."

Samantha smiles knowingly. "I was wondering when you'd ask about that. Yes, the figurine mentioned the sins. But that's just how she *chose* to present the journey. Humans tend to listen more closely when sin is involved—it promises adventure, danger, excitement. But really, it was all a veil. A clever cover for something deeper."

She leans forward slightly, her voice soft but sure. "She called it *lust* when she nudged you toward another man. But it wasn't lust, was it? It was *love*."

Our eyes drift to the ring on my finger. I nod.

"She pushed you to leave a toxic environment, to break free. She stirred up *envy* when someone hit on Ryan—but that wasn't about jealousy. It was about reclaiming your worth, learning not to let others walk all over you anymore. She called it *wrath* when you lashed out at Greg, but it was really the first time you stood up for yourself. You called that trip 'sloth,' but it was the first time you allowed your body and mind to rest, to *detoxify* from everything you'd been through."

Samantha reaches for her tea again, her tone softening even more. "Francine, I don't condone pure evil, true sin. That's not what this was. But the line between sin and self-discovery? It's thin. Messy. Blurry, even. The Woman disguised herself as sin because that's what you needed. That's how you *learned*. Not just what your destination was—but who you are at your core."

She smiles, eyes shimmering. "It's a beautiful journey, isn't it?"

And just like that, tears spring to my eyes—hot, fast, uninvited. They gather and spill before I can stop them.

Samantha grabs a tissue box and hands it to me. "It's okay, dear. This is the final cleanse."

I let it out. Not just the tears, but the weight of everything I've carried. I blow my nose, and with it, expel the residue of my past—the confusion, the self-doubt, the pieces of Greg's voice that still echoed in my mind.

And then... quiet. Sweet, honest clarity.

The fog lifts. The burning questions that haunted me for months dissolve. All the tension in my body melts into the warm chair beneath me.

I exhale fully and smile, eyes puffy but heart light. "I can't thank you enough, Samantha."

She waves it off with a gentle flick of her wrist. "Don't thank me. Thank yourself. You opened your heart. You *chose* to grow. You allowed yourself to discover what true happiness looks like."

I glance around the cozy shop, letting the energy of it settle into me like a new skin. "So... when do I officially take over?"

Before she can answer, the front door jingles. We both glance toward it, surprised—she had turned the sign to *Closed*.

Her husband steps through, arms loaded with bags. "Oh, Sammy girl! I found some brilliant artifacts today—you're going to love them!"

He pauses when he sees me, face lighting up. "Francine, dear! Welcome back."

I smile, lifting my mug. "New antiques, huh?"

He nods, holding up a beautiful, intricate piece of jewelry. A long necklace, its surface dances with brilliant shades of color as it shifts in the light.

"Wow... that's beautiful."

"Isn't it?" he breathes, gazing at it like it's made of stardust. "A princess owned this, centuries ago."

His eyes drift from the necklace to the tissues in my lap, my still-swollen eyes, and finally to the figurine—no, not the *woman of sin* anymore. The *woman of destination*, sitting seductively on the table like she's always known the ending.

He smirks. "So... have we been fully updated, my dear?"

I laugh, dabbing at my mascara with one of the crumpled tissues. "Yes. Fully. She's not a woman of sin, turns out. She's a woman of destination. And I'm taking over the store."

"Yes, love," Samantha chimes in, turning to her husband with pride beaming from her, "she knows now. And I couldn't be prouder of her and everything she's overcome." She turns to me again. "Speaking of... I never answered your question."

She reaches beneath the layers of her clothing and unclasps a necklace I hadn't noticed until now. Nestled between her collarbones all this time is an old silver key. She removes it and places it into my hands.

"This is the key to the store."

Her husband nods, eyes glinting. "It's time. Time for us to live the rest of our lives... somewhere warm. Let's say, Fiji?"

We laugh, and Samantha gives him a playful swat. He grins, then looks at me with such warmth, it nearly undoes me all over again.

"This figurine," he says softly, "she's helped hundreds of people. Me. Samantha. So many others. Humans... we're excellent at losing sight of what matters. We drown in misery. In numbness. In despair. But the lucky ones? The ones who find her? They're guided home. You, my dear, are one of them now."

He gestures to my ring with a wink. "And so is your lucky fella."

"You couldn't be more right," I reply, gesturing for him to take a seat.

He joins us, settling in with ease, like we've been doing this for years. We drink our tea and laugh about the parade of customers who've passed through this shop—each with their own quirks, each with their own story.

It hits me then—really *hits* me—how every one of us thinks we're the main character, the center of the universe, with the world just humming in the background. But the truth is, *everyone is*. Every one of us is a star in our own story. A story shaped by pain, joy, detours, and unexpected teachers.

My story? It's weird. Wild. Unpredictable. Magical. Beautiful.

It's mine.

## TWENTY-TWO

I dust the tables, the antiques, the floor. Dust—nature's most persistent little troll. No matter how many times you wipe it away with a rag or a duster, it returns, shimmering in the sunlight like it's proud of itself before settling right back down. It's almost mocking, like, *"Nice try, sweetheart."* I give the table one more swipe for good measure, then move on to the one in the back.

The sharp citrusy tang of lemon Lysol fills my nostrils as I wipe, and after a few minutes, I straighten my back with a wince. Cleaning day hurts like hell. I catch my reflection in the old mirror—the same one that's been here since Samantha's time. The grey in my hair is more silver now than anything else. I used to dye it obsessively, trying to beat back time with a box of Clairol. But somewhere along the way, I stopped fighting it. You can't outrun dust, and you sure as hell can't outrun destiny.

I set Samantha's infamous kettle on the burner and wait for it to do its thing. I ease myself into the creaky old chair—though it's unclear whether it's the chair or my joints making all that noise. Granny's Treasures has been mine for thirty years now. Samantha and her husband *did* make it to Fiji, just like they said they would. They sent postcards for years, full of sunshine and silly stories. The postcards stopped arriving a while back. I assume… well, I assume they're resting together now. Somewhere warm, I hope.

The kettle starts to whistle and I rise with a groan that sounds like it belongs to a haunted house. I pour my tea, deciding I'll stop at the store on the way home to grab Ryan some Rocky Road—his favorite. He's under the weather today. Poor guy's convinced it's the end every time he sneezes.

I sit back down with my tea, settling into *my* chair—the one where everything changed. I close my eyes, and suddenly I'm back there. Back in ivory lace and sunshine. Back at the altar.

*I watch as Ryan's eyes light up with adoration, love… and a whole lot of tears. He takes me in, standing there in my simple ivory bohemian dress, my hair pinned in an updo with a braid like a crown. His hands find mine and he whispers, awestruck, "Wow, Fran. I have no words."*

*I bite my lip, blushing deep crimson. "Right back at ya."*

*He looks perfect—too perfect. His hair is coiffed just right, his light grey suit pressed like it's been waiting its whole life for this moment. His clean-shaven face glows, but it's his eyes that undo me—hungry, reverent, full of love.*

The officiant turns to the crowd, smiling. "Aren't they just stunning?!"

A ripple of chuckles, then quiet as the room settles into something sacred. I try to meet Ryan's eyes, but bashfulness wins more than once. We exchange vows, his deep voice echoing beautifully. And suddenly it hits me—I'm the bride. I'm her. This is my moment.

He slides the ring onto my finger, slender and sparkling, sealing our promises. When we sign the papers, my heart hammers in my chest. One thought: our first kiss as husband and wife.

We return to the altar, hand in hand. I feel Ryan toying with my ring already—of course he is.

"By the power vested in me," the officiant says, "I now pronounce you husband and wife. You may kiss your lovely bride!"

Ryan wastes zero time. He grabs my face, dips me dramatically, and kisses me like we're in an old movie. Our guests erupt in cheers as I come up for air, laughing. Betty, in a blush-pink bridesmaid dress, claps with tear-streaked cheeks. My mother has her hands clasped over her heart.

We round the corner for a moment of peace before the photo chaos begins.

"Francine," Ryan breathes, taking me in again, "you are the most beautiful woman I've ever seen. You're my wife."

I press against him, feeling the firm lines beneath his suit. "You clean up pretty well yourself, husband."

We kiss softly—until Ryan deepens it, his hand warm on my cheek, thumb brushing against my makeup-covered skin.

"Sorry to interrupt the lovefest!" our photographer calls. She's the same vibrant, quirky woman we adored from our engagement shoot, now peeking out from behind her giant camera. "You two are way too good-looking to not immortalize immediately."

*Our wedding party appears, followed by my mom, who pulls me aside.*

*"Fran..." she starts, eyes glistening, "I am so proud of you. You know that, right?"*

*Tears threaten my lashes again as I wrap my arms around her. "Thank you. And same to you—only true legends beat cancer."*

*"Go on," she smiles, brushing a tear from my cheek. "Go have fun, my beautiful daughter."*

I step back from the memory, heart full and warm. It feels like just yesterday... but decades have passed. The sun is setting now, brushing the horizon like a sleepy kiss goodnight. I consider closing up early to get Ryan his Rocky Road a little sooner—he *has* been a brave little flu warrior today.

That's when I notice her.

A young woman stands just outside the shop, hesitating. She looks early twenties, wearing ripped jeans and a tie-dye long-sleeved shirt with the sleeves pushed to her elbows. A black, worn backpack hangs off one shoulder. Her brunette hair is tossed into a messy bun—the kind of messy that somehow looks cool and effortless.

I always looked like one of the Founding Fathers with my hair in a bun. Especially now that it's practically snow-white.

She seems lost, uncertain. Then she makes her choice.

The door opens with its familiar chime. She steps in and catches my curious stare, cheeks flushing.

"Sorry, ma'am," she says. "Are you closed?"

I cringe inwardly—yes, I *am* a ma'am now. Shaking my head, I point to the door. "The sign still says open, love. What can I do for you?"

She shrugs, eyes wandering around the shop. "I don't really know, to be honest. I was just driving, aimless, and then I saw this place. Something… drew me here. I'm not sure why. I just really don't want to go home right now."

I notice a few bruises scattered on her arms. She quickly moves her shirt to cover them, cheeks coloring.

"What's your name?" I ask gently.

"Rayna," she whispers.

"Nice to meet you, Rayna. I'm Francine."

She offers me a small smile, then starts browsing the shelves. Her eyes catch on the woman of destination, sitting seductively in the same spot I first found her.

"Wow… she's beautiful. Is she for sale?"

Rayna turns to me. I smile.

## THE END

Manufactured by Amazon.ca
Bolton, ON